Gut Reaction

OTHER BOOKS BY KIRBY LARSON

Code Word Courage

Dash

Duke

Liberty

Audacity Jones to the Rescue

Audacity Jones Steals the Show

Hattie Big Sky

Hattie Ever After

Gut Reaction

Kirby Larson
& Quinn Wyatt

Scholastic Press / New York

Library of Congress Cataloging-in-Publication Data available

ISBN 978-1-338-89313-7

10 9 8 7 6 5 4 3 2 1   24 25 26 27 28

Printed in Italy   183

First edition, March 2024

Book design by Cassy Price

For Quinn: *That's one thing done and done well, Mollie Whuppie.*
—Kirby

For my daughters, Esme and Clio, you are my sunshine and I love you more.
—Quinn

Chapter 1

I am bombarded with inspiration: THE ONLY CONSTANT IS CHANGE. WHEN ONE DOOR CLOSES, ANOTHER OPENS. And my personal favorite: IF YOU WANT THE RAINBOW, YOU HAVE TO PUT UP WITH THE RAIN. I'm so due for a rainbow. Unloading a moving van in an October downpour will not make anyone's top ten list. Same for "sleeping" on the floor for a week with your little sister gyrating next to you, ready to play hide and seek at five a.m. Minor complaints aside, I'm glad to be diving into eighth grade at a new school clear across the state. Fresh starts and all that.

The counselor clickety-clicks on his keyboard. "Annnd, print." He rolls his wheelchair around to grab the paper from the printer. "Here you go. One schedule."

Algebra. Science. Language Arts. Social Studies. Pretty much the same stuff I'd be doing back home. "What's SEL?"

"Social Emotional Learning. Talking about feelings and stuff. You'll love Ms. Daley."

Talking about feelings? With people that I don't even know? Oh my frog. I fold the schedule into neat quarters and tuck it into my brand-new planner. Call me old-school.

He pushes away from the desk. "Shall I escort you to your homeroom?"

"Thanks, but the secretary gave me this." Northlake is three times as big as my old school, so I keep a tight grip on the map.

"Hang on." He rummages around in a drawer, then enthusiastically presents a window cling: KEEP CALM AND TITAN ON. "Now you're official. Have a great year, Tess." He waves me off while grabbing his crackling walkie-talkie. Dismissed.

A NORTHLAKE MIDDLE SCHOOL TITAN POWER! banner greets me as I leave his office. DREAMS DON'T WORK UNLESS YOU DO, warns another down the hall. This school flings motivation around like Gracie does glitter. Another poster hangs on my homeroom door: "NO ONE CAN MAKE YOU FEEL INFERIOR WITHOUT YOUR CONSENT." —ELEANOR ROOSEVELT. I hate to disagree with someone like her, but I bet she didn't attend middle school.

I make a wish on my dandelion ring before slipping inside: *New place. New start. New friends?* The teacher's cleaning up a latte puddle on his desk while a tall kid waves his hands around. "Sorry, Mr. Jensen. Sorry, sorry."

"It's okay, Wayne. Accidents happen." Mr. Jensen

pitches a wad of soggy paper towels into the waste bin. "Show's over, everybody. Take your seats."

I hang back, waiting to scope out an open spot. When the scuffling settles, I count empty chairs. Four, but I'm a middle-to-back-of-the-room kind of person so the one in the front row's not happening.

"Here's a seat." A really cute guy points to a desk near him.

A girl with blue streaks in her hair grabs her things and stands up. "Mr. Jensen said I could move there."

"Sorry." I shift out of her way, accidentally whacking another girl with my backpack. "Sorry. Sorry." The goal is to get out of the aisle without maiming anyone else, so I plunk down next to the latte spiller. Nothing like making a grand entrance. I set my pack on the floor and realize no one's even looking at me. Okay. I may survive after all.

The cute guy shows Blue Streak something on his phone. She laughs. He holds it toward me so I can see the photo of two kids wearing Northlake T-shirts. Which is super nice of him but I have no idea why it's share-worthy.

"That was so hysterical." Blue Streak braces her hand on Cute Guy's shoulder, leaning in.

He glances my way and I guess he reads confusion on my face. "Maybe you had to be there?"

I nod. Caitlyn and I used to have tons of inside jokes,

too, before. I never realized they aren't that funny if you're not on the inside.

"Is that a cell phone I see, Mr. Jackson?"

Cute Guy's phone disappears in a flash. "Happy to provide this teachable moment, Mr. J." When he grins, he's even cuter. And probably knows it.

Mr. Jensen nails him with that universal teacher look. "Two more minutes of chat time, sans cell phones."

"That's French for without," Blue Streak offers. "I learned that when we went to Paris last summer."

I learned it from Juliette, the croissant queen at Tony's. Closest I've ever been to Paris.

The latte spiller shifts toward me. "I don't know you." This pronouncement indicates a huge character flaw on my part.

"Today's my first day."

He sticks out his hand. "I'm Wayne Wesley Walker. Pleased to meet you." The words come out all choppy and rushed, like they've been memorized.

I can't leave the guy hanging out there. "Hi, Wayne Wesley Walker. Tess Agnes Medina." We shake.

He points to the floor. "And this is Rexi. Short for T. rex."

A black-and-tan dust mop decked out in a therapy-dog vest looks up but doesn't budge from her spot at Wayne's size thirteen Chucks.

"Hey there, Rexi." I hold out my hand so she can sniff.

"You're good with dogs," Wayne says.

"Well, I had one. Stella. Black lab." Stella was mellow, but she never would've been able to handle the noise and commotion of a school. "Rexi's pretty chill." She stretches out her muzzle and pushes at my hand. I oblige with an ear rub.

"Wait. You said, today?" Wayne pushes his glasses up on his nose. "That must be hard, starting a new school in eighth grade."

"Not as hard as some other things," I say. Ugh. TMI. "I mean, it's okay."

"I think it sounds cool. Living somewhere new." Cute Guy leans in. "We've been here forever." He draws an air line between himself and Wayne. Over his shoulder, Blue Streak zaps me with a glare.

"Mrs. Mulligan wore stoplight earrings." Wayne nods.

"Our kindergarten teacher," Cute Guy explains. "Wayne and I met in that class."

I had friends from kindergarten, too. Like Caitlyn. But after, we just didn't have that much in common. I stuff those memories way in the back of my brain.

When Mr. Jensen's timer goes off, the buzz in the room ratchets down a few notches so he can call roll, which concludes with a "Welcome to Northlake" speech. I want to crawl under my desk when he says, "I expect you Titans to make Tess feel right at home." Thankfully, there's no request to tell the class a little about myself. Then I'd have to join a witness protection program out of sheer embarrassment. The announcements sound pretty much like announcements at my old school: No student pickups or drop-offs in the bus zones. Cell phones will be confiscated if out during class. The student newspaper still has openings for reporters; see Mrs. Chatterjee if interested. Writing is definitely not my marmalade, so I don't bother making a note in my planner.

After announcements, homeroom is a study hall. Complete with no talking. Rexi snores softly while Wayne hunches over a worksheet, erasing as much as he's writing. Looks like square roots. I feel his pain. Give me fractions any day.

Since I don't have homework yet, I unzip my pack for some reading material, pushing past the letter that came the night before we moved. Not ready to deal with that yet. My library book's buried under all the essentials: pens, pencils, phone, lavender lip balm, water bottle, binder. Everything I need to survive middle school except a friend, which obviously doesn't fit in a pack.

The book makes a loud thud when I plop it on the desk. Cute Guy shoots me a look.

"Sorry." I twirl my dandelion ring nervously. "Accident."

He stretches across the aisle and tips up the cover.

"*Bread Science: The Chemistry and Craft of Making Bread*," he reads. "There's a whole book on bread?"

Mr. Jensen taps away on his keyboard. Not paying attention. I turn the page. "Tons of them," I whisper.

"So, it's like recipes?" He takes a closer look. "I bake awesome banana muffins."

Blue Streak tosses her hair, each streak radiating a message: *Don't even think about it.*

I riffle the pages and a Gracie drawing pops out: self-portrait as Noodley Man. Or rather, Noodley Girl. She's obsessed. This is her way of enlisting my help to convince Mom that's what she should be for Halloween. For a four-year-old, she can really plan ahead. I tuck the drawing in the back of the book.

"It's not a cookbook. Exactly." I glue my eyes to the page, hoping he'll take the hint.

"So, what? Exactly?"

He is clearly oblivious to his girlfriend's anti–new girl vibes. "Um. Well." I duck out of Blue Streak's range of fire. The guy seems genuinely interested. "Like about the science of making bread?"

"You're kidding. It's a science?"

I catch myself before reciting Dad's favorite quote about the baguette being the love child of art and science. Stick to the facts. Besides, Dad is dangerous ground. "Yeast feeds off sugar and emits carbon dioxide, which makes the dough rise."

He makes an explosion sound. "My. Mind. Is. Blown."

"Seems like a lot of chatter for study time." Mr. Jensen frowns at us.

Cute Guy grins big—he probably figured out way back in kindergarten that those smiles are teacher kryptonite. Or maybe he's one of those kids who doesn't care about getting in trouble. I am not one of those kids.

I zero back in on the book and discover an entire chapter on brioche. Who knew there were two kinds? Rich man's with a three-to-two flour/butter ratio, and pain brioche with a mere four-to-one. Butter not only makes everything taste über delicious, it also shortens gluten strands. To translate into non-bakerese: Shorter strands equal light and tender. Brioche instead of baguettes, that sort of thing. They are both delicious in their unique French goodness way, but it's the butter that makes brioche sweet and soft and the lack of butter that makes baguettes crusty and chewy.

I wonder what kind of brioche Dad made at his bakery. I always figured I'd have plenty of time to learn.

My hand goes to my middle. Lately, even tiny memories cause a painful gut reaction. Like there's a fledgling in there, pecking to get out. But not a cute little finch like the ones at my neighbor's bird feeder. Something sharp-beaked. Woodpecker, maybe.

Mom thinks stress is causing these stomachaches. Scott, my soon-to-be stepdad, showed me the breathing exercises he uses with people getting MRIs and other major medical stuff. *"Inhale to four, exhale to eight. Clears the mind and sends all kinds of good hormones to the rescue."* Scott has really good advice, so I try it, but nothing good comes to my rescue. Nothing eases the ache. Not in my gut or anywhere else.

The words on the page blur over. Why did I bring a book on baking? Why not one about endangered animals? Or climate change? I'm actually jealous of Cute Guy's algebra homework; he's now lost in solving for *y*. I close the book and study the graffiti on my desktop. Someone's into manga; awesome drawing of Kiki. The bell finally rings and it's rinse and repeat for the next two periods, only with different desk graffiti, motivational posters, and faces. I get friendly smiles, but that's it. Everyone is buddied up; I'm like yeast in a quick bread recipe: unnecessary. I'm guessing my most recent wish is not going to come true.

Third period, SEL, the chairs are arranged in a big circle, all occupied.

"Oh, a new student!" Ms. Daley shuffles papers on her overflowing desk. "I must've missed the memo. Welcome!"

I stand there for half a second before Wayne pulls an empty chair into place next to his. Rexi snuffles in recognition. At least I have a dog buddy.

"Do you like it here so far?" The way Wayne asks his question, I know I have to say yes or I'll hurt his feelings. And he's been so nice. Why bum him out with the truth?

"Sure. It's nice." I get situated in the desk. That's no lie. Northlake's not bad. Just lonely.

Ms. Daley smiles big and asks everyone to tell me their names. It turns out Blue Streak is Tenley Gray, which is a very nice name for an apparently less-than-nice person. Cute Guy is Emmett Jackson.

"All right. Today's lesson." Ms. Daley sets out a glass of water. "How would you describe this?"

A pause and then Wayne offers, "A glass of water?"

"What about the water level?" Ms. Daley hints.

"Oh, I get it." Emmett rocks his chair forward with a thunk. "This is that glass half-empty or half-full thing. Half-full, for sure."

"Half-empty," a couple of kids shout. Ms. Daley doesn't tell them to raise their hands or wait their turn. Just fishes around for a stack of papers from the teetering pile on her desk. "Okay. Let's do a check-in. Fill out this survey using the one-to-four scale. One is No Way and four is That's Me."

The girl next to me smiles. Possible friend material? A wish come true?

"Tess, right?"

I nod. Smile.

She holds out her hand and wiggles her fingers. "Can I borrow a pencil?"

I hand one over from my well-supplied backpack. She doesn't say thanks. Or anything. Maybe she's shy?

A guy wearing a hoodie shoots his hand into the air. "Are you going to read what we write?"

Now I have two people to be grateful for in this class, Wayne for the chair and this guy for the question. I study Ms. Daley so I don't miss her answer.

"Nope." Ms. Daley holds up a finger then points it at the guy. "So be honest, please."

Some of the statements are cheesy: "My future's so bright, I've got to wear shades." But since no one else will see it, I fill out the entire questionnaire. And—no surprise!— score mostly optimist.

When class ends, Ms. Daley hollers over the scraping of chair legs, "Eat a vegetable." That's because next on the schedule is eighth-grade lunch.

You know those stories about the surfer who paddles out too far, nicks her leg on the coral, and the sea around her suddenly roils with sharks ready to move in for the kill? I would trade places with that surfer in a heartbeat. If there is a crueler torture for the friendless than middle school lunch, I can't imagine it.

I pay for my milk, then stand there, scanning for one warm smile. Maybe even a waved invitation to sit. What I get is a jab in the spine with a lunch tray. So much for optimism. I step aside. The jabber—a kid with toilet paper stuck to his shoe—gallops to a table where someone slides over to make room. All around me, kids fan out, finding the sanctuary of a saved seat.

I see Tenley laughing with some friends, and a couple of tables away, Emmett and that kid named Loki are sword-fighting with french fries. Way across the room, there's a table with four girls playing a board game. And a few empty seats. Eyes glued to the splotchy floor tiles, I navigate the vast expanse, stepping around smushed sandwich blobs, dodging a clump of boys playing alpha male, pausing inches from the safety of an empty spot. "Mind if I sit here?"

The girl with Goth nails shrugs.

Close enough to an invitation. I sit. And they get back to their game.

The zipper on my old lunch bag practically shrieks as I undo it. The game girls glare and scoot farther away. I don't blame them.

Where are the sharks when you really need them?

Most everyone around me is talking and laughing. Some kids have their phones out, so it must be okay to use them at lunch. I push aside my bagel and cream cheese and start texting.

> First day of school! Woot! Northlake's gigantic compared to Morgan Middle. I only got a little lost once. Okay, twice.

I insert a goofy face.

> The kids seem okay but they're already kind of grouped up. Don't worry, I won't forget your favorite advice: Be a friend to have a friend.

> Wish you could see the house! Huge kitchen—plenty of room for Bernice. It'll be a good place for baking.

I pause. I want to say, "I miss you." But no sense making anyone feel bad.

> Anyway, lunch is about over so I better go.

I press send even though there won't be any answer.

Chapter 2

The list of rules for Language Arts is long, but I study it like a recipe I'm making for the first time. Tenley clearly spaces out on rule number one because three minutes into class, Mrs. Chatterjee confiscates her phone.

"I was texting my mom!" Tenley flounces in her seat.

Without responding, Mrs. Chatterjee points to the white board. "These are the authors we shall meet together this semester." Her bracelets tinkle like bells as she delivers this news. "Tell me what you know about them." She has a way of looking at you that makes you want to raise your hand. So, I do.

"Louisa May Alcott wrote *Little Women.*"

Those bracelets jingle louder as Mrs. Chatterjee recites: "'I am not afraid of storms, for I am learning to sail my ship.'"

I look at her blankly. Another inside joke?

"A wonderful thought from Miss Alcott. Thank you for that contribution, um"—she consults her seating chart—"Scholar Medina. And welcome to Northlake."

A girl wearing tight braids and a solemn expression jumps in. "Why don't we read anything contemporary?"

"Not this again, Brooklyn." Loki groans.

Mrs. Chatterjee's head tilts. "For example?"

"A graphic novel, like *They Called Us Enemy*, by George Takei." Brooklyn studies the ceiling tile. "Or a regular novel from, maybe, Laurie Halse Anderson or Kekla Magoon or Angie Thomas—"

A boy interrupts. "What's wrong with guy writers?"

Brooklyn doesn't miss a beat. "Or Scott Westerfeld or Francisco X. Stork or—"

"John Green!" Tenley blurts out. "*The Fault in Our Stars!* So good."

Kids name a bunch of other authors. Mrs. Chatterjee writes every single suggestion on the whiteboard. I sit up. Lean forward. We never got to read books by these authors at my old school. This could be the best LA class ever.

I debate raising my hand again to share about the fan letter I wrote to Kekla Magoon—she wrote back!—but suddenly: *ick*. That bird's back at it in my gut. And there's rule number three in red on the whiteboard: *No bathroom passes. Scholars have ample time to take care of personal needs between classes.*

I try breathing the bird away. But it only gets ticked off

and pecks harder. Ugh. Guess I have to break up with bagels and cream cheese.

"Thank you, scholars, for this enlightening discussion." Mrs. Chatterjee replaces the cap on the dry erase marker. "You may certainly feel free to read works by any of these authors. However, the curriculum is already in place for this class." She picks up a worn copy of *Pride and Prejudice*.

Brooklyn mumbles something unprintable.

I'd be bummed, too, if I didn't feel so crappy.

Fifteen minutes left. I can make it. I will make it.

Breathe in four. Breathe out eight. Doesn't help. The woodpecker is mega ticked-off.

Mrs. Chatterjee talks, but I can't hear anything until she calls out over the bell and ensuing racket, "Read the first three chapters for tomorrow."

And I am gone.

I survive the rest of the day. The rain's let up for the walk home, but maneuvering piles of soggy, slippery fall leaves is a workout. I'm a ten-plus on the grouchy scale when I get to our block, but I still wave to our new neighbor, Mrs. Medcalf. She showed up with fresh-baked muffins on our rainy day move-in and we bonded over our favorite English baking show. She's a warm and fuzzy grandma type, even offered to let me borrow her madeleine pans whenever I wanted. But she is too chatty for my mood, so I slip through the front door as quickly as possible. Mom's left a note on the front hall table: *Running errands. Back by 4-ish.* I kick off my shoes, relieved for the reprieve from requests to talk about my day (Mom) and to play Explorer Barbie (Gracie).

After school in the before-time, I'd already be texting with the crew or maybe Caitlyn would've come over to mooch dinner, which happened about once a week, especially when her mom worked double shifts. Then things changed. I don't blame my friends; they tried to figure out the "new" Tess. But I didn't even get myself, so how could they? Easier to do our own things, go our own ways. Easier, but lonely.

While I appreciate the quiet house, I wouldn't mind if Scott was home. He gets me, sometimes more than Mom. Not that my affections can be bought, but he aced it when his proposal included the diamond for Mom, a Bitty Baby doll for Gracie, and Bernice for me: an artisan line KitchenAid stand mixer. Green Apple.

I weave around the moving box obstacle course to flop down on the soft leather of the new couch, backpack and all. Our old sofa didn't make the move, trashed from all the years of curling up with Mom and Dad for Friday movie nights.

My backpack buzzes. I shake it off and snag my phone.

You home safe and sound?

Of course, it's Mom. Who else could it be?
I text back.

> Nope. Kidnapped by aliens.

Ha ha. You okay for another hour? Checking out a studio.

I answer with a thumbs-up.

Be my hero? Empty a box or two?

> Can't hear you. Static.

Smart aleck. Xo

I watch the little dots, wondering if there's more. But they disappear. She probably had to put on the *No No Table Manners* video for Gracie. My little sister has multiple obsessions: That manners video. Noodley Men. Llamas. Arts and crafts. Mom says I was that way when I was four, but the only obsession I remember was wanting to copy Dad.

Another text pops up.

Grab the mail, please? Feel free to lose the bills.

Mom's making this joke a lot lately. Moving costs a fortune, and it's going to take a while to get her photography business up and running here, because people don't know her yet. Scott says it will all work out and not to worry, but he didn't know what it was like for us after, when Mom would wait till we'd gone to bed to cry over our money problems and everything else. The dark circles under her eyes still haven't gone away, not even when Scott makes her laugh. Which is often.

I really should be a good daughter and empty another box.

That woodpecker takes a couple of trial pecks. I rub my middle until it goes back to sleep. Weirdly, these pains started when Mom and Scott announced the move. It doesn't add up. I even get my own bathroom now. No more washing Gracie's toothpaste spit from the sink or moving her potty seat when I have to go. And Bernice doesn't have to live in the garage between bakes. Big plus. Maybe I should make some cookies. Those crunchy oatmeal ones Scott likes. With extra cinnamon to cover up the depressing smell of a house crammed full of unopened cardboard boxes.

For no apparent reason, the scissors are in the fruit bowl. I hunt up the big box marked *Bernice*, and slice through the strapping tape. When I push back the flaps, a memory swoops out, nearly knocking me flat. I can see it playing out right in front of me, like a hologram.

Mom's snuggled on the old couch, a wrapped gift box on her lap. Five-year-old me is plopped on the carpet next to the red stain that's a result of my unauthorized use of nail polish. Trust me on this: Nothing in this universe removes red nail polish from beige carpet. That spot was still there when we moved.

Mom hands me the birthday present and I turn Tasmanian devil, paper flying everywhere. The bow lands on Dad's head.

The first thing I see is the white apron, my name embroidered in red. "It's twins with yours!" I hop up so Dad can tie it on, then I begin pulling out spatulas and whisks and measuring cups and oven mitts, one after another. All perfectly sized for my little hands. "Can we bake something right now?"

"How about a birthday cake?" Dad slips the pack of Doublemint from his pocket—this is a new thing, replacing the cigarettes that were yet another souvenir from Iraq. He pops the gum into his mouth.

"Now?" I am probably the only kindergartner in the world blissed out at the chance to bake her own birthday cake. But that's what Dad does: bake. And I am Dad 2.0.

"You got it." Dad ties on his Tony's Bakery apron.

"Now how will I tell you apart?" Mom asks.

I remember answering very seriously, "I'm the one with a ponytail!"

Mom kisses Dad's shaved head and leaves us to our work. I crack eggs. Weigh flour. Unwrap sticks of butter. Even start the mixer. I do it all. Except the oven, which is a grown-up job. Don't get me wrong: That cake was delicious. But the best part was whipping it up.

With Dad.

I back away from the moving box and scare up some Kleenex. Why are these memories causing meltdowns now?

Easy answer.

And it's in my backpack.

I close the flaps. "Tomorrow, Bernice. I promise."

My bed's an island floating in another sea of boxes. Owlie perches on the pillow, watching me with unblinking eyes. I park next to him, cross-legged, tug open the backpack zipper, and pull out the envelope. "Just because they sent it, doesn't mean I have to answer, right?"

Owlie keeps his opinions to himself.

"You're not a lot of help." I straighten the used-to-be-green scarf around his used-to-be-white neck. Not that I needed to read it again, but I slide the letter from the envelope, open it up, scan the page.

Dear Former Bake-Off Competitor:

For the tenth anniversary of the Jubilee Flour Junior Baker West Coast competition, we're hosting a Best of the Best Bake-off in Portland, Oregon, inviting all former competitors since the contest's inception. And that means you!

The theme is Spring Dreams, and the judges will be "cooking up" a variety of surprise baking challenges. Entries will be judged on creativity, presentation, and, of course, taste.

This special contest promises a special reward for the winner: a spot on the hit show Frosted Junior, *with an all-expenses-paid trip to Los Angeles, and a chance for the $10,000 grand prize.*

I skim the rules. There are the usuals, like following safe and sanitary baking procedures and using only Jubilee Flour, of course, because they're the sponsor. Also, participants must audition with a video and, if that's accepted, get judged by a local professional baker in order to make it to the Portland competition in April. Before I can glance away, my eyes catch the handwritten note at the bottom, and I'm teary all over again. *Sure hope you'll say yes. Marie Chang*

"What do you think, Owlie?" I grab another Kleenex.

He stares at me with big button eyes.

The advice I want is not going to come from Owlie. I pick up my phone. Type in the details about the bake-off.

> I don't want to stress Mom out. There's the entry fee. Gas $ to get there. Hotel room + practice supplies.

The woodpecker is going nuts, tapping out warnings as I text. I rock on the bed to soothe it.

> **What do you think I should do?**

I hit send, knowing what the answer would be. And that makes me use up another fistful of Kleenex before I can get a grip. Finally, I stop crying. Wash my face. One of Mom's superpowers is that she can spot old tears a mile away. And she's got enough to worry about.

I start to pitch the letter, but Owlie's eyes burn a hole in me. So, I neatly refold it and stick it in the bottom of my sock drawer. "Happy?"

He doesn't make a peep in reply. But I swear I catch a whiff of Doublemint.

Chapter 3

After a couple weeks, the game girls don't even glance up from the board anymore when I sit down. They take turns drawing tiles and building kingdoms as I spoon baby bites of my vanilla yogurt. The game has room for five players, but they don't seem inclined to invite me. When Goth Girl argues with Glasses Girl about whether it's better to complete a city or a road, I shift forward to share a strategy tip I learned over the weekend. Before I can speak, they're on to raving about the haunted house they went to on Saturday night. As Scott likes to say, "Too slow, Joe."

I rummage in my lunch sack for the crackers I packed and discover some of Gracie's Halloween candy. She thinks I must be devastated that I didn't get to go trick-or-treating, so she keeps sharing her loot. I learned the hard way on Halloween night that the woodpecker does not care for KitKats. And the last thing I want to do is break one of Mrs. Chatterjee's rules since I'm not doing that great in LA. I wish I understood what she wanted. I thought teachers liked it when you wrote down the stuff they said in class. But my first essay assignment got branded with a big C minus and the comment *What does Tess think?* underlined in purple.

I can't even catch a break with the required weekly journal entries. She says they're good practice for the final essay (fifty percent of our grade) and that they build "muscle memory for the left side of the brain." Maybe I'd do better if she didn't find her prompts at the Walmart of Language Arts. The last one was "I wish," which is something that Gracie's preschool teacher might come up with. Not that I don't wish for things. Who doesn't? But I'm not about to write them down for someone else to read. Even thinking about it starts the gut-pecking. Besides, what I ended up with was good; it was about how I wished Elon Musk would get his Hyperloop tunnel built because it would help people be with their loved ones and help with the climate and traffic jams. *Personal connection?* was the only note in the margin. Along with that familiar purple check-minus.

I pitch my yogurt cup and Gracie's candy and head for LA where Mrs. Chatterjee is writing this week's prompt on the board: *Why I love to . . .*

Finally, a prompt with possibilities. I dig out my pen.

When we're all seated, she announces that today she'll look for volunteers to share their responses. I wish I could figure out how she does that with her voice. She's like a siren in Greek myths whose sweet songs lured sailors too close to the rocks. When she asks you to do something, you really want to. Maybe she's a hypnotist?

Anyway, I start writing, safe in the knowledge that I will resist the siren voice, no matter how many extra points it costs me.

Why I love to bake is a question I can answer in two words: my dad.

I sit there for a sec, waiting to see what the bird in my gut will do. A few tiny angry pecks but bearable. My pencil flies over the page. *I know a lot of kids think their fathers stash a superhero cape in their closets but mine wore his every day. A starched bleached chef's coat with his name embroidered on the front. He showed me that a few ordinary ingredients can be combined to make something to brighten a sad day, mend fences, grant wishes. I love to bake because he loves to bake.*

I sit back and re-read it. Ta-dah. Personal connections. Guaranteed purple check-plus.

The timer goes off and Mrs. Chatterjee scans the room, grade book in hand. "All right, scholars. Who's my first volunteer?"

Tenley holds her right arm up with her left, as if it's dead weight. Mrs. Chatterjee calls on her, and she shakes her blue-streaked hair and clears her throat. "Why I love to travel. Because last summer we went to Paris and Zurich and I got to hang out with my cousin Ainsley and meet boys from cool places like Austria and eat Toblerone chocolate every day. We finished our trip in Rome where we went to the Hard Rock Cafe. I loved the trip so much, I went old-school and sent postcards to my friends at home." She peeks over the top of her journal at Emmett. Obviously, one of the postcard-receiving friends.

"Rome might be my favorite city. The Sistine Chapel. The Coliseum. The Trevi Fountain. I must confess that I've never been to the Hard Rock Cafe there, however. Thank you, Scholar Gray." Mrs. Chatterjee makes a note in her grade book. Her face lights up when she sees Wayne raise his hand. "Scholar Walker, are you volunteering?"

Wayne is a tree when he stands—tall and stiff—his face so white with nerves that all I can think is *Timber.* At least the two people in the front row look strong enough to catch him. He wobbles a bit and I close my eyes; can't watch. But he rallies. Finds his footing. "I love to build obstacle courses for Rexi," he begins. "It's fun to figure out how different pieces could fit together. Like a huge jigsaw puzzle. And Rexi may be small, but she isn't scared of the teeter-totter like some bigger dogs. You should see her run up and ride it down. Mostly I love to build courses because I would do anything for Rexi because she is everything to me."

Mrs. Chatterjee blinks and makes a mark in her book. She coughs into her hand. "Thank you, Scholar Walker. Wayne." I swear she wipes away a tear.

"That was really good," I tell him when he sits down. "Rexi liked it, too."

The dust mop wags her tail when she hears her name. "Obstacle courses," I tell her. "Who knew?"

"She needs work on the weave poles," Wayne confesses.

Rexi huffs as if this flaw is not even worth mentioning. I can't help laughing. Out loud.

"Are you volunteering, Scholar Medina?" The question hangs in the air like burnt sugar.

"No. I was just —"

Mrs. Chatterjee taps her grade book, a nonverbal reminder that I could use the points. Her tinkling bracelets can't sway me. I shake my head. Stare at the desktop. More manga: Sailor Moon this time.

Brooklyn raises her hand. "I'll go."

Does Mrs. Chatterjee twitch? "Perhaps we could give another scholar an opportunity?"

But no one raises a hand, all of us probably wondering what Brooklyn's going to say this time. She is the definition of perseverance.

"Scholar Tanner." Mrs. Chatterjee's smile doesn't move beyond her lips.

"Why I love the ALA and their list of best books for young adults." Brooklyn looks at Mrs. Chatterjee. "That's the American Library Association, the oldest library association in the world." She's like one of those TV lawyers entering a piece of evidence in a trial.

"I am aware of the ALA." Mrs. Chatterjee's expression about makes me pee my pants. How is Brooklyn so gutsy?

"I also love the work of Donalyn Miller, The Book Whisperer." Brooklyn glances down at her journal. "Ms. Miller says, and I quote, 'If we want children to see reading as anything more than a school job, we must give them the chance to choose their own books and develop personal connections to reading, or they never will.' The end."

Mrs. Chatterjee sighs as she makes a note in her grade book.

Brooklyn and I end up heading out together after the bell. "That was like *Law & Order* in there," I say.

"Fat lot of good it did." She tugs on her backpack strap. "I guess we should be grateful we're at least reading a few women writers. Dead ones, but still—"

"Mrs. Chatterjee has kind of left it open for the future . . ."

Brooklyn gives me the side-eye. "You probably still believe in Santa Claus."

"Just the Easter Bunny." That earns me a smile before she dives into the stream of kids heading one way and I dive into the stream heading the other.

Chapter 4

Mom's in the entry, fumbling with her purse. "I got another lead on a studio. Shouldn't be more than an hour or so."

"What about Gracie?"

"Where are my keys?" She shoves her hands into her pockets and comes up empty. Another rummage in her purse. "Okay. Got 'em. She can watch *PJ Masks*."

"Mom."

"Or take her to the library."

"I have homework." I'd had the whole walk from school to fume over Mrs. Chatterjee's comment on my Why I Love To entry: *Don't assume the reader knows that simply because your dad bakes that's why you love it. Explain! Flesh out! Personal connections.* That's triple underlined in purple. Purple check-minus. I give up. I am so going to flunk LA.

"An hour! At most. Dinner's in the Crockpot." And, like a pear-and-freesia-scented hurricane, she's out the door.

I slam it behind her. The noise pulls Gracie and her stuffy Mr. Monkey away from the TV. "Can we?" She bounces Mr. Monkey up and down. "Go to the liberry?

Llama Llama Red Pajama!" She turns her request into a chant.

My backpack thuds to the floor. "I just got home. I don't want to go anywhere." I want to hide out in my room. Scream into my pillow. Search for essays I can buy off the interwebs. Not entertain a four-year-old.

"*Llama Llama . . . ,*" she sings louder.

"Stop it."

Gracie spins and twirls, volume increasing with each 360. Now she's shouting at the top of her lungs.

"Shut up! Just shut up." I've yelled at my sister maybe two other times in my life. And now I remember the reason why I don't. She drops Mr. Monkey, scrambles away, and buries herself under the throw on the couch. There's no crying. No hysterics. This is a million times worse.

"I'm sorry, Gracie. I didn't mean it." Her little tush pokes out from under the blanket. I sit on the couch and pat it once. "Come on out."

Her head wobbles back and forth.

I stroke her blanketed back. "I'll take you to the library."

Her head emerges. "Can I get *Llama Llama*?"

"If they have it."

She emerges from her blanket cocoon and lets me tug her onto my lap, the top of her head notching right under my chin. I used to sit on Dad's lap just like this. "I'm really, really sorry I yelled."

She exhales with a shudder. Through the T-shirt, her ribs spell out a warning in Braille: tiny child, huge emotions. "I don't like it when you get mad at me."

"I don't like it, either." I kiss her head. "Hey, maybe we can bake when we get back?"

"Chocolate chip?"

I round up her tennies. "Good choice. Dad's favorite."

She grabs the shoes. "Help me?"

"See if you can do it yourself, first." Family rule.

She crams the left shoe on to her right foot. "This way?"

"Other foot."

She looks down. "No, this is right."

At least it's only a few blocks to the library. Though the bathrooms only have half doors on the stalls. But there are bathrooms. First thing I look for in new places these days.

"You like to bake because of Dad, huh?"

"Remember how good he smelled when he got home from work?"

Gracie clomps to the front door in her wrong-feet shoes. "No. But he brang me gummy worms."

I'm gut punched. "That's Scott."

"I like the red ones." It doesn't seem to faze her that she's mixing them up. She tugs the front door open, discussion over.

"You need a coat. Unicorn or pink?"

"Unicorn."

I wrangle her into the unicorn raincoat, not ready to let it drop. "Dad gave us gum. Doublemint."

"I'm not 'lowed to chew gum." She skips into the November drizzle like a born Pacific Northwesterner. I hunch up my shoulders against the rain for the second time that afternoon.

"Oh, hi, ladybug. We're going to the liberry. To get *Llama Llama*." She crouches down, settling in for a conversation.

"You can chat with ladybug later." She doesn't fuss when I take her hand. It's warm and so small. I squeeze it three times.

"One, two, three!" She squeezes back.

"That means 'I love you.' We learned that from Dad." I practically shout, as if saying it with enough volume will bring it all back to her. I tighten my hold as we cross the street. "Don't you remember?"

She shakes her pigtails. "Nope." There is no regret in that answer. No longing. She *was* little when it happened. But still. It's our *dad*! And Gracie thinks he brought us gummy worms.

When I was little, before I knew better, I'd plop the cookie cutter smack in the middle of the rolled-out dough. Dad showed me how to go around the edges instead, to get more cookies. But he's not around to show me what to do about that Dad-shaped hole cut out of the middle of my heart.

Gracie skips ahead.

"Slow down!" I don't really care that she's ten steps

ahead of me. She's got street sense. It's more about my missing Dad when she doesn't seem to. I try one more time. "Do you remember—"

"Look! A baby bear!"

I swallow down the rest of the question, along with my jealousy that Gracie's every thought of Dad isn't an oven burn.

She runs to a sculpture outside the library's front door and scrambles up before I notice the sign.

"That says no climbing." Trying to tug her off is like trying to peel an Ariel sticker off a brand-new planner.

Her pout disappears when we discover story time in progress inside. She marches over to a little boy wearing an animal puppet on each hand, severely violating his personal space. "Can I play?" She slips her hand into the turtle puppet he offers.

Of course, to a four-year-old, making friends is as easy as sharing a couple of puppets.

Gracie's turtle puppet is swimming around the little boy's clownfish. "A shark! Run!" She zooms her puppet away, the clownfish right behind. Normally, her imagination cracks me up. But it's hard to shake off the idea that she's completely forgotten Dad.

"Is everything okay?" A grandmotherly lady pushing a cart full of books pauses.

Oh my frog. What vibes am I giving off? Get a grip. "Um. Can you tell me where the computers are?"

"Over there."

In plain view.

I wipe at my eyes. "Allergies. Thanks." I force so much cheerfulness into my voice, it's amazing I don't cause a sugar overdose. The lady pauses a moment longer, then rolls on.

The librarian has corralled Gracie and her new buddy and they're sitting, criss-cross applesauce, with a gaggle of other little kids, listening to *A Visitor for Bear*, another Gracie favorite. The librarian's decent at the voices.

I sit down at the closest computer, open the browser and, without letting myself think about it too long, type in the search bar.

Up pops the page for the Jubilee Flour Junior Baker Competition. There's Chef Marie's photo, right next to the "Tenth Anniversary" logo. A few strands of white in her hair but the same kind eyes. To avoid those eyes, I scroll through the site. A couple of other photos pop up. There's one of that girl from Oregon. Maren Taylor. She helped me make a new batch of buttercream frosting when I overbeat the first one. And there's Simon Nguyen, who even made the crabby judge laugh with his jokes. Looks like he's grown about a foot. He was a wizard with fondant.

The librarian's voice is background noise as I click. Bear is looking in the fridge to make sure Mouse has really gone. Getting near the end of the story.

I scroll back to the home page, cursor over the button

that says, *Download an entry form*. The little white glove icon hovers over *entry*.

I can't.

Instead, I pull my phone from my pocket.

> Took Gracie to story time. Nice library. Of course, she's already made a friend. Her superpower.

My thumbs hover over the phone. Making friends is not my superpower. But I do have one: baking.

> Do you think I should just print off the entry form?

"Look in the teapot!" Gracie squeals.

"Teapot!" echoes her new friend.

The story time kids jump to their feet. "I told you!" Gracie's voice is triumphant. I glance over. She does a clumsy high-five with her new friend before they run back to the puppets. She embraces her superpower. And I know Dad wants me to embrace mine.

With one eye on my sister, and one eye on the screen, I click download. And then, print.

A few minutes later, we're on our way home. Gracie carrying *Llama Llama Misses Mama* in her arms. Me carrying my future in my pocket.

Chapter 5

On the Monday before Thanksgiving break, Wayne's desk is empty. Around me, people are chatting about their holiday plans. "I hate pumpkin pie," Tenley's saying. "Oh man, I could eat one by myself," Emmett tells her. I'm Team Emmett on this. With no one to go over my Thanksgiving plans with, I pull out my newest library book, *Flour Water Salt Yeast*. Guess I'm getting the hang of going solo through middle school. Definitely sucky, but doable. I'm in the middle of a section on fermentation when the classroom door pops open. "Hey, Mr. Jensen!"

"Elly! I forgot you were coming today." Mr. Jensen motions in a pair of students. One of them is Brooklyn. The other girl has long straight hair pulled back in a sleek ponytail. "Come on in."

"Hi, guys!" Ponytail waves. "Well, I'm Elly Liu—"

"Elly P-U," I hear Tenley mumble.

"—and this is Brooklyn Tanner. We're from the International Club and want to personally invite you to our bazaar next Friday during lunch. It's going to rock! Music and crafts for sale and did I mention crafts for sale?"

Elly's being a goof but she carries it off, bopping around, emitting positivity. "And now heeere's Brooklyn with the details."

Brooklyn holds up a handful of flyers. "We'll have tables from around twenty different countries so there's going to be something you love. All the money goes to Doctors Without Borders. A really good cause."

Tenley waves her hand. "Are the club members making the crafts?"

Brooklyn sets a flyer on Mr. Jensen's desk. "Most are being donated."

"Because some people make stuff that's tragically bad." Tenley looks straight at Elly.

"I know. Right?" Elly doesn't blink. "Worst macramé-er ever. That's why I'm in charge of publicity." Game, set, and match to Elly Liu.

"Any questions?" Brooklyn looks around the room. "Okay then. Bring your money next Friday and prepare to shop till you drop."

Elly waves both hands and makes an adorkable face that no one else could pull off. How does someone get to be like that? All sunny and snark-proof? I could use some of those vitamins she's taking.

SEL goes long, and I'm late to the cafeteria. While I'm in the lunch line, I catch sight of a dark ponytail across the room. Elly Liu. But there's someone else next to her. A guy.

I head for my usual spot at the game girl table and poke at mashed potatoes and turkey gravy. My stomach vetoes this menu choice and I head for the second-floor bathroom; not that it was urgent this time, but because of Mrs. Chatterjee after lunch. Best to plan ahead. And that's the bathroom with the smallest chance of running into someone crying, rolling on lip gloss, or hiding out to text their BFs. The bathroom visit doesn't help. The woodpecker's invited some friends to move in; too many sharp jabs for one beak.

I move like molasses on the walk home, almost in slow motion and cautiously, as if I'm carrying a soufflé so it doesn't fall. The jabbing forces me to stop a couple of blocks from home. Am I going to heave right here on the sidewalk? Oh my frog. So much pain. This is no flock of birds. They've moved on, replaced by a porcupine with laser-sharp quills. I'm barely holding it together when I pass the Medcalfs' yard and Peanut's *stranger danger* alert system kicks into high gear. Mrs. Medcalf's with him, but I can't hear her over his yapping.

She picks him up and rubs his ears. Finds his off button. "From all that racket, I was certain we were being attacked by aliens. Or zombies."

I plaster on a smile. Peanut's a cute little guy, with that black pirate patch around his left eye, but oh that annoying bark. Good old Stella hardly ever let out a woof. Labs are like that.

I should say something nice. No matter what, people love their pets. "He's quite the watchdog." I edge away. Need to get home. Almost there.

"My best boy!" She gives him a squeeze. "Did you catch the show last night? Victoria sponges!"

I try to rock without rocking. "I know. The jelly roll part looks tricky."

"Maybe we could tackle it together."

"Sure. Yeah." I start toward our house.

"Oh, hold on. I cut out a recipe for you." Before I can say anything, she disappears inside. Some deep breathing quiets the porcupine; I'm almost normal when she returns with a newspaper clipping. "Thought you could bake these for your friends."

If she only knew. I take the clipping. "Thanks."

"Say hello to your folks." She kisses Peanut on the head. "And tell Gracie I hope we can have that tea party soon!"

Only a few bills in today's mail. That should chill Mom out. Along with finding a studio space. She's a happier camper when she's working.

A glass of water seems to tame the porcupine. Note to self: Drink more water. I'm feeling a ton better, so I put my stuff down, grab a glass of water, and read the recipe. Salted butter oatmeal chocolate chip cookies. Sounds like ultimate goodness. And I could sub out the chips for raisins in half the dough for chocolate-hating Scott. I gather up the ingredients and when I see some coconut flakes in the pantry, I grab those, too. Why not?

I insert Bernice's flat beater then hunt up the scale and measuring spoons. Dad taught me to weigh out everything. No sloppy two cups of flour or half stick of butter for me. You can go so wrong that way! A cup of sugar is 200 grams, but a cup of honey is 340. No wonder so many people resort to mixes.

When the dough's ready, I divide it and add chocolate chips to one part and raisins to the other. Both versions smell heavenly as they bake, but a taste test is required before I can pass final judgment. I break two still-warm cookies in half and take a nibble of each. I'm a chocolate girl, but the raisin ones are right up there. Nine and a half, even.

In the before-time, when I had friends, I used to have to whack them with the wooden spoon to keep them from devouring my bakes. Especially Caitlyn. That girl could seriously put away the sweets. But then, who doesn't like cookies?

A cartoon lightbulb goes off above my head. Because, duh, who doesn't like cookies? Nobody. Maybe the game girls would warm up if I brought treats. I fix up four cute packages of cookies and tuck them in my pack. When Gracie bursts through the door and launches herself at me like a bottle rocket, I swing her and Mr. Monkey around, feeling lighter than I have in a long while.

I set her on the floor, and she wobbles before regaining her balance. "Guess what?" she asks.

"I give."

With a hand to her mouth, she stage-whispers, "Mom found a studio."

"Can't wait for you to see it!" Mom follows, juggling two bags of groceries. I grab one.

"Cookies!" Gracie shows Mr. Monkey the plate.

"After dinner," Mom and I say together. Mom laughs as she opens the fridge to put away the milk and eggs. "How was your day?"

The truth would stress her out. Anyway, my life is about to change. I rinse the bunch of grapes and eat a couple before putting them in the fridge. "Tell me about the studio."

We get to hear about it all over again at dinner. The light. The funky vintage couch. The great parking.

"To Sarah Medina Photography!" Scott clinks his wineglass with Mom's.

"The best part is, I can start moving stuff in this weekend."

"Can someone cut my trees?" Gracie waves around a broccoli spear.

"Oh, babe." Scott reaches over to do the cutting. "Remember? I have that training?"

"Shoot. I forgot. All weekend?"

"'Fraid so."

"I can help." Pitching in at Mom's studio is nothing new. Same with helping Dad at the bakery. I like being useful. And it's not like I have big plans. Or any plans.

Mom makes a face. "I was hoping you'd sister-sit you-know-who."

Gracie interrupts. "Knock, knock."

"Who's there?" Scott's a sucker for Gracie's jokes.

"Figs." She's already cracking up.

Scott's eyebrows waggle. "Figs who?"

Gracie bounces in her chair. "Figs the doorbell. I've been knocking forever!"

We all laugh. Scott's is genuine. Mom and I are pretty good at faking it. Gracie tries out a few more jokes, which get progressively unfunnier, then we talk about a bunch of stuff—thankfully, not about school. And I help Scott clear the table before bringing out the cookies.

"Can I have two?" Gracie presses her tiny hands together as if she's saying a prayer.

"They look pretty rich."

"I ate all my trees." The kid should be a lawyer.

Mom takes a bite. "Whoa. Really good. But only one." This to Gracie. She turns to me. "New recipe?"

"Mrs. Medcalf thought I'd like it." I eye the cookies, but my gut gives the no-go signal.

"What's the secret ingredient?" Scott asks. "Arsenic?"

"What?" My forehead crinkles.

"I mean, you're not eating any."

"I taste-tested." Normally, those two sampler bites would've been two sampler cookies. At least. Evidently, porcupines are not cookie fans.

"Tea?" Mom fills Scott's mug and offers me some.

"I almost forgot." I hold out my cup. "Mrs. Medcalf said she hoped she and Gracie could have that tea party soon." I stir in some sugar. "Maybe she'd be willing to watch Gracie for a few hours this weekend, then I could help you?"

Mom blobs some milk into her mug. "Seems like a lot to ask . . ."

"Well, she brought it up," I point out.

"I'll call her later." She sips her tea. "Great thinking, Tess."

Two good ideas in one day. Things are starting to look up.

Chapter 6

"Pizza or totchos?" The lunch lady waves her spatula between two equally unappetizing options. The pizza resembles decorated cardboard. And I'm not sure Buffalo chicken totchos are technically food.

Anticipating the answer, she slaps pizza on my tray. I pick up a carton of milk and some baby carrots with ranch dressing. Which, have you ever read the ingredients on that stuff? I make it from scratch. Cheaper and sans the unpronounceable.

The cashier scans my ID card.

In four. Out eight, I breathe.

Fueled by good endorphins, I approach the game table and set down my tray. Goth Girl's face relaxes into a softer scowl when she sees I'm minus the noisy lunch bag. One point for Team Tess. It's now or never.

"I made a new recipe yesterday." I pinch my ring as the words race out of my mouth. "Would you guys like to try? Salted butter oatmeal chocolate chip."

Glasses Girl's head pops up.

"Um, I don't take food from people I don't know." Goth Girl turns back to the game.

You know *me*, I want to say. I've been sitting at your table all this time.

"Yeah. Stranger danger," adds Braces Girl.

Glasses Girl eyes the cookies. "They look professional," she says.

I'd thank her for the compliment, but she's already rolling dice.

The pizza makes me want to puke. My gut reaction is to head for the garbage cans to pitch my uneaten lunch. And the cookies.

Then, out of the corner of my eye, I spot her.

Elly Liu.

The bubbly and positive Elly Liu.

Talking to a boy with an equally friendly face.

They look like people who might eat cookies without worrying about stranger danger. I could walk over there and ask. Just. Walk. Over. There.

Stupidest move ever, my gut tells me.

Be a friend to make a friend, my heart counters.

If they laugh, you'll have to skip lunch for the rest of the year, my brain chimes in.

But Elly doesn't seem like the laugh-at-you type, my heart points out. *What do you have to lose?*

Everything. My gut and brain are in complete agreement.

But my heart takes charge. And, somehow, I'm standing next to Elly Liu.

"Hi, Elly from the International Club."

Her eyes light up. "Do you want to join?"

"Actually, I was wondering if I could join you for lunch." I hold up the paper bag. "I come bearing cookies."

"Get this person a seat!" The boy yanks his jacket from the stool and pretends to brush it off. "Rajit Gupta."

"Tess Medina." I try to keep my cool as I sit.

"Ah." Elly nods. "Tess Agnes Medina."

How does she know my whole name?

"Show-off." Rajit tosses a totcho in her direction. "Are you new?"

"I started mid-October."

"Newish." Elly opens her yogurt. "I'm plain Elly Lui. No middle name."

"Cool tee," I say.

"Mine or hers?" Rajit dips a carrot into the ranch dressing minefield. He's wearing a plain red shirt.

"Um. Hers."

Elly glances down as if she has no idea that she's wearing an autographed Brandi Carlile tee. "Tess Agnes Medina, critical question." Her face grows serious. "Lighthead or Ten Elephants?"

The right answer may mean an end to loner lunches. "What are the parameters?"

"I like your style."

"You may have met your match." Rajit sticks a straw into a carton of chocolate milk.

"So?" Elly raises an eyebrow.

"Well, King Green for 'Opportunity Knocks,' but Saving Tanya for 'Vampire Love Letter.'"

"Unconventional answer." Elly leans back, appraising. "But please don't tell me you listen to LonelyDog."

Six of their songs are loaded on to my favorite playlist. "I plead the Fifth."

"Aggh." Her head drops to the tabletop. "And you had so much potential."

Is she being sarcastic?

After a few beats, her head pops back up. "Wait. I see it all now. You've come for a reason: So I can give you a proper musical education. Vinyl is where it's really at." She fishes her phone out of her pocket and scrolls to a photo of an album cover. "You have to come over and listen to this."

We've only met and she's inviting me over? "Sure. Yeah. That'd be great."

Rajit points to his ears as if they had buds in them. "She gave up on converting me. Strictly musicals."

"Which are awesome," Elly inserts. "But it doesn't hurt to expand your horizons."

"Believe it or not, I've heard this lecture before. Perfectly content the way I am." He manages to eat the messy totchos without getting any Buffalo sauce on himself. "So, did you read Tess's student files or something?"

Elly scrunches up her face. "What?"

"Tess Agnes Medina," he reminds her.

"Oh, I get it. That's all Wayne. My neighbor." Elly scoops some yogurt.

"Stoplight earrings," I say.

Elly's brow wrinkles, confused, then she nods. "Those made a big impression on him. Anyway, he told me about you. You made a big impression, too."

"He's sweet. And I love Rexi." I glance around the cafeteria. "Where are they?"

"This chaos and Wayne are not a good mix," Elly explains. "He and Rexi eat lunch in the music room. You should hear him play the piano. A-mazing."

"I bet he solos in Benaroya Hall someday. Anyway, about me," Rajit says. "Elly and I met last year."

"He was standing by his locker, looking lost." Elly presses her hand to her cheek. "What can I say? I'm a regular Girl Scout."

She reminds me of Gracie, with that easy way of making friends.

"Combination locks are a seventh grader's worst nightmare." Rajit dips another totcho. "She had to open mine for, like, a month. Combinations." He shakes his head.

I poke at congealed pizza cheese. "I wrote mine on my hand so I wouldn't forget."

"Locker problems rank up there with these." Rajit flashes his braces. Miraculously, food-free.

"And PE," I add.

"Actually, what *is* good about middle school?" Rajit asks.

"Us!" Elly claps her hands.

My stomach somersaults. Am I an "us"?

"So, what are your other classes?"

I tell her. When I mention Mrs. Chatterjee, she jumps in. "If you like Jane Austen, you'll be fine."

We're nearly finished with *Pride and Prejudice* and I'm still not sure if I like Jane Austen or not. "How about you?"

"Big fan."

"I don't mean Jane Austen, I mean, what's your schedule?"

"I'm in honors. Raj too. Hey." She glances at my tray. "Do you always buy?"

I set my fork down in defeat. I cannot do this pizza. "Depends."

"Do not under any circumstances order the chicken nuggets." She shudders. "I got so sick on those last year."

"Duly noted."

"So, Tess the Trainable, tell all." Rajit points a carrot

toward me like a microphone. "How did we come to be blessed with your company?"

I slide the straw up and down in the milk carton. "You like cookies?"

"Yes. And as you can also tell, we are so popular, we have to fight off the hordes desiring to share our table."

"It's a big problem." Elly snitches another totcho from Rajit's tray.

Rajit glares at her, then looks back at me. "Our listeners are dying to know. What is Tess Medina's real story? Hopes and dreams? Hobbies?"

My hopes and dreams are to survive eighth grade, but that sounds pitiful. "I like to bake."

Elly grabs my arm. "Double fudge brownie mix!"

I suppress a shudder, but I'm not about to bake-shame a possible friend. "That's good, for sure. But I'm more into homemade." I shake the cookie bag, inviting them to try.

Rajit rips into a packet and makes nom-nom noises. After his first bite, he smacks the table. "You *made* these? Like, from a recipe? Measuring and stirring and stuff?"

I nod.

Elly sighs as she crunches. "And you share your talent with your friends?"

"The best part of baking is sharing."

"Will you sit with us every day?" Elly's bitten the cookie into a smile shape, which she waggles my way.

My own smile is my answer.

"Can I have your phone?" Elly punches in her number. "Now what's yours?"

I give it to her, then take a bite of cold, soggy pizza. It's delicious.

Chapter 7

The drizzle on the way home dampens my hair but not my spirits. I read the note Mom left on the kitchen counter: *Took Gracie with me to the studio. Home around 4:30.* Below that, Gracie drew a wonky sun with blue crayon—or maybe it's supposed to be me; hard to tell with four-year-old art. I stick the picture on the fridge with a magnet then dig out my phone.

> Hey! I took your advice and I have a friend. Two friends!

Well, may have two friends. Okay, to be precise: I didn't have to eat lunch by myself today. I count that as a win. I add a smiley face and hit send, then break out some ridiculous dance moves. I wouldn't even care if someone saw me. Much. Best day ever. I shimmy around the room and realize I'm hungry! Actually hungry. Warm rosemary sea salt pretzels coming right up. Dad's favorites.

Good baking requires background music. I set my Pandora station to Linda Ronstadt—the album Elly had shown me—and flip open my recipe book. Lots of people store their recipes in computer files, but I'm old-school. Paper planner, paper cookbook. There's something soothing in typing out each recipe and it makes it easier to double-check the ingredients. Plus that's what Dad did. I pause at the only handwritten page in the whole book: the recipe for Joyful Cookies. I run my fingers over the tidy block printing, reading the dated notes. Dad never could stop tinkering. My heart cracks when I read, *Per Tess: add macadamia nuts. Next time.* I lean close to the page, inhaling deep, and swear I catch a hint of Doublemint. It was this recipe that earned me a spot in that first bake-off competition. He'd been so proud of me. After I made it to the final round, he said he'd have to change the name of the shop to Tess and Tony's. I pat the smudged paper. I may suck at writing essays, but I can bake.

A few more pages in, I find the pretzel recipe; it's scribbled over with notes, too. I guess I really do take after him. One note reads, *Cheese sauce missing something?* It had been kind of bland last time. Maybe add a hint of paprika?

The water, sugar, yeast, and melted butter get dumped into a bowl for five minutes. After that, I throw in the salt, rosemary, and flour and start Bernice on low. No offense to Linda, but I'm going to need a different beat for kneading. Queen Medallion does the trick; I crank up the volume then set the dough on the counter and find my rhythm. Knead, quarter turn, knead. Dad always said he did his best thinking when he was up to his elbows in flour. With my hands occupied, my brain starts demanding some attention.

Dad found a way to make the bakery happen, my brain says. *You can find a way to make the bake-off happen.*

There's a little thing called money, I remind my brain. Right before the move I cleaned out my savings to buy an ice-cream-maker attachment for Bernice. With Mom taping together her torn light umbrella, no way can I ask her to chip in. Used to be, if I needed money, I'd call up Michael and Trent. With four kids under five between them, they paid double for a sitter. Sometimes triple. Of course, I miss the kids, especially little Lachlan, but the boost to my savings account sure was sweet. Maybe I could put a sign up on the bulletin board at the library: BABYSITTER. LOTS OF EXPERIENCE.

Decision made, I pat the dough into a soft-as-velvet ball and tuck it in an oil-rubbed bowl just as the phone rings.

Scott is old-school when it comes to phones. 911 can't pinpoint locations from cells and he doesn't want to take any chances. We're probably the only dinosaurs in town with a landline.

"Oh, there is someone home," Mrs. Medcalf says. "The house looked dark."

"I'm back in the kitchen." I cradle the receiver between cheek and shoulder to cover the dough with a damp towel.

"I'm completely out of baking soda, can you believe it? Do you have two teaspoons I could borrow?"

I check the cupboard. "Yep."

"I hate to ask, but could you bring it over?"

The dough's got about an hour to rise. "Sure. Give me one sec." I measure some soda into a little glass prep bowl and throw on a hoodie.

I don't know how she hears me knock over Peanut's yapping, but the door swings open. "Hush, Peanut. I mean it. Be quiet." He doesn't hush or be quiet as she holds him back with a booted foot.

"What happened?"

She grimaces. "Twisted my ankle. Only a sprain. But it hurts like the dickens. Peanut, knock it off." She pushes him back inside as I hand over the dish of soda.

"I'm baking thank-you cookies. I fell right in front of the fire station, if you can believe it. At first, I thought the only thing I'd injured was my pride." She waggles the booted foot. "But I managed to do a number on this. And, of course, Gary's out of town for the next couple of weeks." She looks over her shoulder at Peanut throwing himself against the screen door. "No walkies. Poor little pup."

"I could take him. Would that help?" I owe her something for the cookie recipe.

She presses her hand to her chest. "You are a lifesaver."

"I have some time right now, if that works."

"My gosh. Yes." She opens a drawer and pulls out a leash and a handful of poop bags, which I'm used to because of Stella. Then, she pauses before handing over the stuff. "Oh, and no argument. I am paying you."

"It's okay." Mom will have a fit if I take money from a neighbor.

"Then I can't ask you to do it." She grabs the leash back.

I think of the bake-off. Take a deep breath. "What if I walk him for free today, as a trial, and if it works, you could pay me. Like, for a couple times a week?" I duck my head. "I am trying to earn some money."

"You've got yourself a deal."

Peanut bounces around like a Super Ball, tangling us both in the leash. He forgets he's only about eight inches high and barks ferociously at squirrels, skittering leaves, even an old guy with a German shepherd. I have to admit, his take-charge attitude cracks me up.

"Macho dog, huh?" The old guy chuckles when I tug on Peanut's leash to keep him from pouncing on the shepherd. Our Stella earned a Canine Good Citizen award; I'll bet Peanut's never set one paw inside an obedience class.

Ten minutes in one direction and ten back should give Peanut a reasonable amount of exercise and get me back in time for the pretzels. After he calms down, he walks two whole blocks without yanking my arm out of the socket. Then: Squirrel! Game over. He launches into attack mode, flopping and jerking like a fish on a line. I pick him up, stroking between his eyes and down his muzzle to calm him. "I don't blame you. Those gray ones don't even belong here." We'd learned about invasive species in science a couple years back. The gray squirrels moved west, kicking out the native Douglas ones, taking over their habitat, and eating all their food. You only saw the Douglas squirrels in the woods. If you were lucky.

"Hey, Tess!"

Wayne heads toward us with Rexi. I stop and wait. Peanut does his fish-on-the-line routine, acting like he'll explode before Rexi gets close enough to say hello.

"I didn't know you had a dog." Wayne signals Rexi and she sits like a charm. Peanut bounces around her like an oversized flea looking for a place to jump on.

"My neighbor hurt her foot so I'm walking Peanut for her." I rub Rexi behind her ears. "You are such a good girl."

"So, you're a dog walker?" Wayne asks.

I lure Peanut away from Rexi so she can have some breathing room. "I guess. For now."

"Rexi has her Canine Good Citizen certificate," Wayne says.

"So did my old dog, Stella." I look down at Peanut. "Peanut's not so big on good manners."

"I can sort of tell. No offense."

"None taken." I pat Peanut in case our conversation hurts his feelings.

"I gotta get going. See you at school." Wayne gives Rexi another signal and she trots along, at his heel. In the meantime, Peanut's twisted his leash around his two back legs.

"You goober. Come on. We need to pick up the pace." I give a gentle pull on his leash and ease into a slow jog. His little tail and ears perk right up. "You like this, don't you?" I do, too. Brings back memories of running with Dad. I'd prefer him to Peanut as a running partner, but it feels really good to move. To breathe deep. To push myself.

I step hard off the curb, and something shifts in my side. That's what I get for being such a couch potato since the move. Peanut's still raring to go, but I slow to a walk, breathing into the twinge. That usually does the trick. This time, the pain expands, like one of those sponge toys in a glass of water. I press on my stomach to keep it from growing too big. It doesn't work. The porcupine is on a rampage. Was it the pizza? Or thinking about Dad? Whatever it is, I need a bathroom. Like, immediately. And the last two blocks stretch out like twenty miles. I'm going so fast that Peanut's tongue flops out. But I can't stop.

There's no time to drop him at Mrs. Medcalf's. I drag him to our house, into the bathroom. He rests his muzzle on his front paws, looking worried, while I sit on the toilet, shaking from pain.

Finally, the diarrhea stops. I wobble to the sink to wash my hands and press a cold cloth to my face to stop the tears.

Oh my god. That was horrible. What if I hadn't made it home?

Peanut whimpers to be picked up, so I do, slowly, gently, so the porcupine doesn't get ticked off again. "Sorry I freaked you out," I whisper. He licks my cheek tentatively as if he's not sure he can trust me. We make it to the front entry bench and sit there trembling together. "I better get you home." I feel a thousand years old when I lean over to set him down and pick up his leash. The walk next door is a marathon.

"Everything go okay?" Mrs. Medcalf asks.

"Yeah," I answer, thankful Peanut can't tell her the truth. Luckily, her favorite talk show's blaring in the background so she heads back in without chatting.

Our house is still empty. All I want to do is lie on the cool tile kitchen floor until the dough finishes its rise. So that's what I do. And mentally add school pizza to my "do not eat" list.

Ping.

I reach for my phone.

Whatcha doin?

Elly!
I wobble to a sit, tenting my knees.

Waiting for pretzel dough to rise.

U were serious about that baking stuff.

Her text dulls a few of the porcupine quills. I answer with a smiley face.

Can u bring me one tomorrow?

They're better fresh.

I'm not picky. Please! 🙏 **Besides, I need something to cheer me up. Student Council might not have enough $ for the eighth-grade graduation dance. Trés bummed.**

Sorry.

And I am because that porcupine is prickling again, with ice pick quills digging at my guts.

It's a tradition! 😠 They spent too much on the portable planetarium last year. That's why.

The ice pick jabs again. I catch my breath before I answer.

Double sorry.

I've wanted to be on the dance committee since I was in 6th grade!

Triple sorry.

I'm now rocking in place. Am I going to be able to stand? Get to the bathroom in time?

Gonna figure out how to make it happen.

U will.

😃

Sorry. Gotta go.

Homework?

Yep.

It's only a little lie.
She sends me a barf emoji.

Almost appropriate.
Wrong end.

Chapter 8

"Sounds like you had a great time at your cabin." I settle on the stool next to Elly. I'd been stressed out over Thanksgiving break, worried that I'd misread her friendliness, even though she'd texted me a bunch of times. But as soon as I got out of the lunch line, she'd jumped up and directed me to their table like someone guiding an airplane up to the gate. It was only mildly embarrassing. "It's so cool that Brandi Carlile's your neighbor up there."

"Do not try to cheer me up." Elly slumps over a bowl of tomato-basil soup. "Not in the mood."

"What's wrong?"

"Two words." She shoves the bowl out of the way and plunks forward on the table. "Michele Meyer."

"Hey, Tess." Rajit slides into the seat opposite.

Elly turns her head. Glares. "What am I? Chopped liver?" She should definitely be in drama.

"And hello to you, our little unicorn of happiness." Rajit dips his head in acknowledgment, then leans across the table to speak to me. "Is there a reason for this despair?"

"Michele Meyer?" I guess.

Elly's upright again, poking at her soup with a spoon. "I'd hate her, but she's über sweet."

"I'm not tracking this conversation." Rajit unwraps a burrito.

"The day can't get any worse," I explain.

Elly grabs Rajit's arm. "She sat by Dylan in Student Council this morning. And talked with him!"

"Talked? Or 'talked'?" Rajit asks.

A sharp exhale riffles her bangs. "Oh, I don't know. But he laughed. Three times! And then walked her to class after."

"Well, Dylan Yoon is a friendly guy. And tall. Really tall."

"I think I've seen him in the halls. Dark hair. Wears old-school Vans. He's cute. I can see why you like him," I add.

Elly makes a squeaky hamster sound. "I didn't say I like him!" She flaps her hand. "Whatever. Oh, and the other thing is that there is absolutely for sure no money left in the budget. Adios, graduation dance."

"She's wanted to be on the dance committee since sixth grade," Rajit explains.

"I know. Sorry." I point to a nearby poster. TOUGH TIMES DON'T LAST. TOUGH PEOPLE DO.

She snarls.

"There's only one cure for such tragedies." I hand her a small paper bag from my backpack.

She rips it open. "Cinnamon rolls! That'll work."

"To be completely accurate, orange-glazed cinnamon rolls."

Rajit fake-pouts. "Are there any for tragedy-free people?"

I hand over a bag for Rajit, too. "They're better warmed up, but I couldn't figure out how to do that."

"We have our own Cat Cora. Right here at Northlake Middle." He licks orange glaze from his fingers.

Elly polishes off her first roll then folds over the top of the paper bag. "I'm saving this one for after school."

"Warm it in the oven, not the microwave." I spoon up the applesauce that had been the only appealing cafeteria offering. "Otherwise, it gets rubbery."

"Okay. I am serious here." Elly swivels my way. "Can you teach me to bake something? I can't even boil water."

"Everyone can boil water." Elly and her drama-rama.

Rajit shakes his head, a sorrowful expression on his face. "I regret to inform you that she is one hundred percent correct. One time we were baking those refrigerated cookies—"

"—Where all you have to do is slice the dough." Elly pulls out the second roll and takes a bite.

I bury my face in my hands then peek at her through my fingers. "Do you know what those are made of?"

Elly wrinkles her nose. "Clearly carcinogens are delish."

"Anyway, as I was saying"—Rajit clears his throat—"our brainiac here decided to speed up the process."

"Not my best moment," Elly admits.

"Do you know what you get when you bake cookies at 500 degrees? An oven fire. Complete with firefighters." Rajit grins. "That part was cool, though. One of them was really cute."

I wonder how a person in honors can do something so brainless, but I'm not going to say that out loud. "Maybe it was beginner's bad luck?"

Elly nods vigorously. "I'm sure that was it."

"Dylan sighting." Rajit lowers his voice.

Dylan Yoon looms over us, eyeing Elly's roll. "Where are they selling those?"

"Nowhere. They're home-baked." Elly's answer sounds remarkably hamster-like. "Would you like one?" This with a questioning look at me. Luckily, I brought extras. I kick my pack toward Elly and she pulls out another paper sack.

Dylan munches. "This is amazing."

"It's even better warmed up," Elly and Rajit say at the same time.

"And don't even think of doing it in the microwave," Elly warns.

"There's not going to be anything left to warm." Dylan

polishes it off. "Man, El, this is almost as good as those fancy chocolate chip cookies you made."

Rajit coughs.

"Glad you liked them." Elly could win at professional poker with that face.

"I could eat about a dozen of these."

Rajit protects his sack. "They're all gone."

Dylan sighs. "Bummer."

Elly strikes a diva pose, back of hand to forehead. "All good things must come to an end."

"Okay. Well, later." Dylan wanders off.

"When did you make chocolate chip cookies for him?" Rajit pretends to fall off his stool. "And how did he survive?"

"Well, I shared one of Tess's cookies and he somehow got the idea that I baked them."

"Somehow got the idea?" Rajit wags his finger. "I wonder how."

"I might've omitted a few key details." Elly's voice trails off. "He really liked them."

"I can give you baking lessons. Then you won't have to omit 'key details.'" I use air quotes. "Bernice is getting rusty. She could use a workout."

"Bernice?"

"My KitchenAid stand mixer. Bernice."

Rajit and Elly stare at me, open-mouthed. Oh my frog. They think I'm weird.

"My mom's been drooling over them for years. They cost a fortune," says Rajit.

"Well, it was a gift." They don't seem too weirded out after all.

Elly shakes her head. "You have your own mixer?"

I push the foil lid back over the applesauce cup. My do-not-eat list gets longer every day. Even the smell of applesauce brings out the porcupine quills. "I like to bake. I even—" I stop. Too braggy?

"You can't leave us hanging." Elly tugs my sleeve. "You even . . .?"

What happens if I tell them? Will it open doors I won't be able to close? What if there are questions about Dad? "Oh, nothing." I play with my ring.

Elly's face is as serious as a final exam. "There's no 'oh, nothing' with friends."

Friends. I never noticed how that word sounds like a granted wish. Or answered prayer. "Okay. A couple years back, I was a finalist in the Jubilee Flour Bake-Off."

"What?" Elly throws her arm around my neck. "You're famous!"

"Not famous." I wiggle to get free but can't escape until she loosens her grip. The girl is strong.

"Our little star." Rajit frames my face with his hands. "What did you bake?"

"My own invention called Soda Shoppe cupcakes,

topped with Whoppers. They taste like a chocolate malt." The porcupine's now a sharpened knife. Quick jab. I cover the gasp with a cough. *Inhale four. Out eight.* I don't know if it's the lunch or the memories bringing this on.

"I'm practically drooling." Elly smacks her lips.

"You had me at Whoppers. Best candy ever." Rajit sips his chocolate milk. "And you didn't win with that amazeball cupcake?"

I open a mental Ziploc bag, stuff the bake-off memory inside, and seal it tight. "No."

"Well, that's a bummer. I'd have given you the prize if I'd been the judge." Rajit crumples his milk carton. "But you know the bigger bummer? Dylan's going to blab and, pretty soon, we'll have to share Tess with everybody."

"Well, we found her first." Elly shoots me a quick look. "Not that we only love you for your baking skills. Your taste in music is severely above average."

When I laugh, the porcupine eases off. My gut feels almost normal. "I'll always share with you guys."

"So, you'll give me baking lessons?"

"Anything for love." I try hard to lighten my voice to match the words.

Elly does a wonky seated happy dance. "You. Are. My. Hero."

"What about me?" Rajit crosses his arms.

Elly blows him an air kiss. "You are both my heroes."

"I mean, I'm feeling excluded." He gathers up his lunch trash.

"Do you want to learn to bake, too?"

"If that's what my friends are doing, yeah."

Even though Rajit's pouting, I can't help smiling. A wish. A prayer. "Group lesson," I promise.

I can't wait to text Dad.

Chapter 9

"You're finally here!!!" Gracie launches herself at Elly as if they go way back. "Did you bring me a present?"

"Gracie!" Mom gasps.

"What?" Gracie asks. "It's practically Christmas."

"This is going to be a long month." Mom sounds exasperated, but she laughs.

"It's okay." Elly produces a small drawstring bag from her backpack. "Ta-dah!"

Gracie drops Mr. Monkey to loosen the ties and peeks in. "A troll!"

"An original." Elly slips out of her jacket. "It was mine when I was little. Maybe even your age. I named her Woodsie. But you can call her whatever you want."

"Woodsie! Woodsie!" Gracie twirls the doll by its pink hair. "Wanna play Pioneer?"

Elly checks with me. "Do I?"

"Maybe later, okay? She just got here."

"I definitely need help hanging the wreaths. How about it?" Scott taps Gracie's shoulder.

"Can I pound the nails?"

"That's why I got you a kid hammer." He reaches for her hand. "Come along, buddy."

I wave Elly to follow me to my room before Gracie changes her mind.

"Your sister is adorable." Elly gives my bed a test bounce. "Hey, I kept my old Ramona books, too."

"'Sit here for the present.'"

Elly wears a blank expression.

"That's what the teacher tells her when Ramona starts school and—" I remind her.

"Yes! She sits there waiting and waiting and never gets a present. Totally forgot." Elly straightens the photo on the wall. "Your grandpa?"

"He lives in Arizona."

She pats it and moves on, checking out my room like it's a museum exhibit. "Things were so confusing when we were kids. Like when Mom said she had cold feet about something, I brought her slippers. She still laughs about that."

"What do you mean things *were* confusing? They still are!"

"I hear ya." Elly plunks down in front of my bookcase and squeals. "Candy Land!"

My stomach gets squidgy. I should've removed such embarrassing artifacts before she arrived.

"Best. Game. Ever. I have the Winnie-the-Pooh version."

She slides it off the shelf, opens the lid, and pulls out the game tokens. "Whoa. These are custom."

I ignore the growing pressure in my stomach. "Yeah, well. My dad made them."

"Want to play while we wait for Rajit and Wayne?" She starts setting up the board before I have a chance to respond. "Can I be this one?"

Dad's piece. "Sure." I set the candy cane on the start square. That was always mine. Mom's was the slice of cake. "Company goes first."

Elly shuffles the cards. "I hated that rule when I was a kid. Except when I was company." She squares up the pile of cards and turns over the first one. "Purple!" The gingerbread man taps along the board.

We go back and forth for a few more turns. The porcupine does not wait its turn. I can't hold it any longer.

"Be right back!" Thankfully, it's over quickly. But I open the bathroom window after. Note to self: scented candles. I return with snacks, as if that's why I'd ducked out.

"I suppose you made these?" She grabs a cookie.

"Homemade chocolate cherry bars. So easy." I put one on a napkin for myself.

"Easy for you!"

She wipes off her hands and takes her next turn.

I grab a card, ignoring the porcupine's persistent jabbing. Until I can't. "I'm thirsty. Want a drink?"

"Sure."

Elly doesn't comment on how long it takes me to come back with the water. "You have got to listen to this!" She hands me an earbud.

A deep voice fills my head. Warm. Powerful.

"She's good," I say.

"Nina Simone." Elly sighs. "A-mazing singer. And out-there activist. Civil rights and stuff."

"Sounds interesting."

"Interesting!" Elly rolls her eyes. "Try fascinating. Complicated. Fierce."

I roll my eyes right back. "I didn't realize I had to write a report on her."

"Why am I friends with you again?" she asks.

"Baking lessons?" I lower my voice. "Dylan Yoon?"

She sticks her tongue out.

"Very adult." I turn over the next card. Purple.

"Thank you." She nods her head like a queen acknowledging her subjects. Draws a card. Red. "Where the heck are those guys?" She texts Wayne and gets a quick reply. "Oh, Rexi got into something and is . . . um, indisposed. They can't come. I'll check with Raj." A few seconds later her phone pings. "It's his weekend at his dad's. And a bunch of family showed up. He can't come, either."

"That's too bad. Green." I move my piece. "Not that he's with his dad, I mean."

"Do you switch weekends, too?"

"Switch weekends?"

"Between your mom and dad? You say 'Scott,' not 'Dad.'" Elly wraps her arms around her knees. "Too personal? Sometimes I don't know when to shut up."

She bumps the board, then fumbles around, straightening the fallen pieces. "I hope it was friendly. When my auntie and uncle split, they seemed happier. He still comes to all our family stuff. With his new wife, even."

I check in with my gut. The porcupine's pulled in its quills so I answer. "Um. My parents aren't divorced." I should've also checked in with my heart, which starts leaking out my eyes.

She grabs a tissue and hands it over. "I'm sorry. Not my business." She leans back to grab a tissue for herself. "I'm a sympathetic cryer."

"It's not like it's a deep, dark secret. Just sad." I shudder-sob. "Everyone tells me it's not my fault, but my dad died alone in a grocery store parking lot. All because I needed more Whoppers."

Elly plunks the entire box of Kleenex between us. "I'm listening."

I only mean to tell her the bare minimum, but it all bubbles out. Well, everything but the texting. "It's been three years, but I can still hear Chef Marie asking me to come with her." I blow my nose. "Everyone was so kind, even the police officer. Said it wasn't my fault. But I was the idiot who'd run out of Whoppers. If I hadn't done that stupid extra practice bake, I would've had enough. And when Dad had the heart attack, he wouldn't have died alone in an IGA parking lot." The words come out like a wail and I have to stop talking for a while to catch my breath.

She tosses another used Kleenex on the pile. "It's not your fault."

"I know." I do know. And I don't. "It's complicated." I hold out my hand. "He gave me this ring that morning. Said he hoped all my wishes would come true." That starts us both blubbering again. Finally, I get enough of a grip to tell her about the tenth-anniversary competition. By the time I finish, there's a three-tiered Kleenex wedding cake between us.

"You've got to do it." Elly blows her nose again. "The bake-off."

I crumple another Kleenex. "I know what you mean. For my dad."

"No, for you. It's unfinished business, like Jimi Hendrix's *Black Gold* album."

"That is way over my head."

She flaps her hand. "Doesn't matter. The point is you're a type A person—"

"Hey, thanks."

"I mean that in the nicest way. The attention to detail is

what makes you a good baker, right? That's a good kind of type A, in my book."

"Forgiven," I say.

"You gotta do it. Let's download the application form right now." She hops over the used tissues.

"Already done." I pull it out of my sock drawer.

"Why haven't you sent it in? Do you need a stamp? We can borrow one from my mom."

"I've got stamps. And enough for the entry fee." Thanks to Peanut.

Elly grabs the form. "Then let's get this puppy in the mail."

I grab it back. "It's not only the entry fee. There's gas money to get to Portland, hotel, food. And all the supplies for practice bakes. Trust me, it adds up."

Her forehead wrinkles. "But you have that dog-walking gig, right?"

"Elly. A hotel costs over a hundred dollars a night." I've already said more than I meant to. Might as well be totally honest. "The other thing is that I'm pretty rusty. I kind of got out of the habit after . . . everything. And five months isn't much time to get ready."

She processes this, sitting perfectly still, something I've never witnessed. Elly-lost-in-thought is a whole different creature. Like the eagle I'd watched when we stayed by the ocean once. It perched in a nearby maple tree, a feathered statue, then—whoosh!—it was airborne. And within seconds, an unsuspecting mouse dangled from its talons. I couldn't shake the feeling of having something in common with that poor rodent right now.

"Okay. Here's the plan. First, you are an incredible baker. It'll be like falling off a horse or whatever. Second, I can be your sous chef—do bakers have those?" She doesn't wait for the answer. "I'm a research phenom and can dig up hard recipes. Three, we'll bake every weekend. By we, I mean you. I know Rajit will help. Wayne too." She sits back, looking completely pleased with herself. Problem solved.

"There's still the money," I remind her. "And Mom."

"If you can earn the money, will your mom say yes?"

"Ninety-nine percent sure."

After another eagle minute or so, she stirs. "Time to put this out to the universe. Repeat after me: *Tess needs money for the bake-off. Tess needs money for the bake-off.*" She kicks my foot with hers. "You're not repeating."

"Because it's ridiculous."

"Say it!"

"Do I have to refer to myself in the third person?"

That question earns me a snort.

"Okay. Okay. *I need money for the bake-off. I need money for the bake-off.*" After ten more recitations, Elly seems satisfied that we've fulfilled a sufficient quota of universal requests. And I don't feel like crying anymore.

The bedroom door slams open. "What are you guys doin' in here? Ooh, Candy Land! Woodsie loves that game." Gracie pretends to feed her the cake token.

Elly scoops up the pieces. "We weren't very far along. Which piece does Woodsie want?" Her phone pings. "Let me check this." As she reads, her eyes open wide. Her mouth, too. "You. Have. Got. To. Look. At. This." Her hand wobbles as she holds out the phone. "It's from Wayne."

> Do you have Tess's number? My gramma needs a dog walker. So does her neighbor, Mr. Jackson.

My head inflates like a helium balloon.

Elly has Wayne on speed dial. And, in about five minutes, I have two new clients: Mr. Jackson's Ruffles and Mrs. Taber's Trixie. Oh my frog. I inhale, sniffing for Doublemint. Did Dad have anything to do with this? Then I come back to earth. Elly's going to be impossible to live with.

"The universe sure believes in fast service! You better ask your mom. Soon."

"Ask Mommy what?" Gracie asks.

"Dance party!" Elly cranks on "Let It Go," and we all

shake it up around the room. Elly and Gracie compete to see who can hold the last note the longest.

Elly faceplants on the bed, panting. "I give." Clearly, she has some experience with four-year-olds.

Gracie waves Woodsie all around. "I win! I win!"

"Enough celebrating. We want to bake, right?" Elly tugs Gracie's ponytail.

"Mom said I could watch *Paw Patrol*," Gracie's voice trails off. "If I don't help, do I still get a cookie?" Her new favorite story is about the Little Red Hen.

"I say heck yeah," Elly says.

"Absolutely," I add.

Gracie skips off and we follow.

"She's adorable," Elly sighs.

"But kind of a pain when it comes to baking."

"Unlike me." Elly pulls a bright orange notebook out of her backpack and sets it on the kitchen counter.

And she calls me type A? I consult the recipe. "Weigh out 270 grams of flour."

"But what about these?" Elly holds up two glass measuring cups.

I fake-shiver. "First, those are for liquids. Not dry ingredients. And second, you get better results when you weigh."

"My grandma doesn't. She throws in handfuls of this or that."

I fold my arms across my apron. "Then get Grandma over here."

"I guess I'll learn how to weigh." She scoops out flour and dumps it in the bowl, pressing down with the spoon.

"No pressing! Dump it back and start over."

"Man, you're picky."

"Do you want cookies or hockey pucks?" I ask.

"Hang on a sec." She turns to a fresh page in her notebook. "No pressing the flour," she repeats as she writes.

"This is going to take all day," I grumble. But it doesn't. We even have enough time to whip up a batch of salted caramel blondies. When her mom comes, Elly floats out to the car, carrying a container of cookies like it's pure gold. "Mom. Look at what I made. All by myself. And no firetrucks involved."

As they pull away, Elly hangs her head out the window. "Be ready to work next weekend!" she hollers.

"I've created a monster!" I holler back, waving until they take the left onto the main drag. I realize I've eaten two cookies without disturbing the porcupine. Elly is good medicine.

Bernice waits on the counter, ready to go. I pick up my phone.

I need lots of practice. Start with crème pâtissière? Or work on my Swiss buttercream. I'm also rusty on macarons.

I catch a whiff of Doublemint as I remember that macarons are Chef Marie's favorite.

You got it. Macarons.

I'll start right after I mail the application.

Chapter 10

I pull on my hoodie and bounce down the porch steps. Next door, Mr. Medcalf is braced on a ladder, hanging tiny white lights from the eaves. Mrs. Medcalf untangles green strings as Peanut runs back and forth between the two of them. Mrs. Medcalf waves. "Off to see Ruffles?"

"Word gets around," I say.

"No secrets in this neighborhood!" She hands one end of a strand of lights to Mr. Medcalf. "I play canasta with Mr. Jackson."

"I like your decorations." I zip up my hoodie. Maybe I should've worn another layer.

Mr. Medcalf shakes his head. "I usually get them up Thanksgiving weekend and here it's the middle of December."

"Better late than never," says Mrs. Medcalf. Peanut yaps as if he's disagreeing and they both laugh.

It does seem like they are the last people in the neighborhood to Christmas up. Miss Patti's Daycare is a red-and-green explosion, and down the block there's a yard filled with inflatables that Gracie drools over every time we pass. The house next door to it has planted a big Grinch sign. Kind of funny.

When I get to Mr. Jackson's porch, I knock, "shave and a haircut," like Dad would. Deep woofs reverberate through the wooden door. Ruffles. I was nervous when I first met her because she's enormous but, also, definitely all bark and no bite. And lots of slobber.

The door opens. "Hey." Emmett.

I back up. This is the right house. Yellow shutters, blue welcome mat?

"Gramps said you were coming. Come in."

Gramps?

Mr. Jackson joins us in the entry hall. "I hear you two know each other from school."

"She's a science wiz." Emmett grins.

I stand there, twisting my ring, wishing I could vanish. "So maybe you don't need me today?"

"A deal's a deal." Mr. Jackson clips Ruffles's leash to her collar. "Besides, my girl's full of vinegar this morning. A real handful."

The "handful" is flopped on the floor, impersonating a shag rug. An enormous shag rug. "I can see that."

"Don't let her fool you." Mr. Jackson rubs her side gently with his slipper. "One sight of a squirrel and it'll be hang on for dear life."

Emmett starts through the door, then turns back. "Dog treats?"

"Got it covered." I tug on the leash, but Ruffles is anchored. "Walk? Treat?" One of the words connects and she morphs from rug to dog. Shakes. I dodge most of the slobber as I cookie her and we're off. "I thought I'd take her to Carlyon Park."

"Sounds like a plan." Emmett pulls the door shut behind us, which opens a large chunk of sticky silence. I'm thrown off-balance seeing him out of context. Trying to think of something to say is like trying to get glue off my fingers.

"Your grandpa is nice." Ruffles sways at my side, a big black ship of a dog sailing down the sidewalk.

"He is." Emmett takes an air shot. "Used to be my basketball coach."

I loosen the leash so Ruffles can water a patch of weeds. "Oh. You play basketball?" I should give lessons, I'm such a brilliant conversationalist.

Another air shot. "Did." He bounces on his toes. "I'm into track now. Do you do a sport?"

"Leave it." I scold Ruffles as she sniffs a Mickey D wrapper. "Is baking considered a sport?"

"The kind you do might be, Ms. Bread Science."

"I come by it—" I stop myself. "Bakers run in the family."

"I'm jealous." He kneels to tie his shoe. "Mostly accountants in mine. My mom can't bake a chocolate chip cookie to save her life."

"Don't stereotype," I say.

"You should be Elly's debate partner." He smiles. "Has she driven you bonkers yet with her music?"

As if she has ESP, my phone pings.

Wait till you listen to this!

I show him the link. Rockabilly! "She *is* pretty intense."

"Intense doesn't cover it. In kindergarten, it was dinosaurs, 24/7. Second grade, she was going to save all the elephants." He pulls a pack of gum from his pocket. Offers me a piece. Thankfully, not Doublemint. "Sixth grade was the worst. Germs. It got so I could barely eat my lunch."

"So you guys go way back?" I blow a little bubble.

"Our moms were in a baby class together." His words are wintergreen-scented. "You want to meet Mabel?"

"Do I?"

"Definitely." He starts down a gravel path through a thick stand of trees. "This way."

Ruffles sniffs every plant and shrub; she's in no hurry. I wonder how Emmett knows Mabel is around. We're in the middle of the woods.

When we reach the Y in the path, Emmett hesitates. "Um, so there's something I wanted to talk to you about . . ."

Something tells me it's not going to be about baking. "O-kay."

He picks up a couple of pinecones and starts to juggle. "So I know about your dad."

"What do you mean?" I jerk Ruffles's leash harder than I intend. I thought I could trust Elly.

"Um. Well. Grandpa and Mrs. Medcalf are good friends."

"They play canasta." Whatever that is. And now I am thoroughly confused.

"Mrs. Medcalf told him and that's why Gramps asked me to come over today." He drops the pinecones. Brushes off his hands. "My dad died, too."

My anger dissolves. It wasn't Elly. I expel the breath I've been holding. "When?" I can't help asking.

"Five years ago."

"What of?"

"Cancer."

I pause. "Three. Heart attack." This is like a tennis match, batting bad memories back and forth across the net. "I'm really sorry about . . . everything. But do you mind if we change the subject?"

"No. But if you ever want to talk about it—" Emmett's voice softens. "I'm here."

I think about breaking down with Elly. Is it still like that for Emmett? Or by the time you get to five years out, can you piece together the broken parts of your heart like torn pie dough? Do the memories stop stomping on your soul? I sneak a glance. He looks like someone I could talk to. And maybe I will. Someday.

"I appreciate the offer. Thanks." I wrinkle my nose. "Are you okay if we don't talk about it any more now?"

"You got it." Ruffles pounces on the wood chips that skitter her way when Emmett scuffs his feet. "But if you change your mind . . ."

I press my lips together as something occurs to me. "Did you tell Tenley?"

He shakes his head. "It feels weird that I know."

Yeah. Me too. Tears push at the backs of my eyes; how do I get out of this?

Ruffles saves the day by doing her business at that very moment. I put the poop bags to use, taking advantage of the distraction to change the topic. "So, Mabel?"

Emmett seems relieved, too. "Not much farther." He takes off.

Ruffles picks up the pace, and I jog behind, panting when they stop in the middle of a big clearing.

"Tess, meet Mabel." Emmett pats an enormous tree trunk.

Even doing a back bend, I can't see the very tiptop. "Whoa. That's, I mean, *she's* tall." I press my free hand to the coarse bark. It's cool. Damp. And calming. I kind of want to lean in, soak up some of that calm.

"And six hundred years old. Maybe the oldest tree in

the area." He kneels to brush back an overgrown fern, uncovering a worn brass plaque. Ruffles flops at his feet; I lean over her to read it.

"Douglas fir. Started growing around 1400." That triggers memories of social studies discussions about the first peoples in the Northwest. "Do you think a Salish kid planted her? Or Tlingit?"

Emmett rubs his sweatshirt sleeve across the plaque to spiff it up. "Hate to burst your romantic bubble but it was probably a squirrel."

"Please say it was an awesome prehistoric one, at least."

"Whatever." His laugh is like fresh-out-of-the-oven bread slathered with butter. "Can you see that gnarly knot up there?" He stands up to point.

I squint. "You mean the mole on steroids?"

"Yeah. That's a burl. Not real attractive on the outside. But beautiful on the inside. My dad made bowls from them."

"I love wooden stuff. I have an old dough bowl that was my great-grandma's. Not from a burl, though. What causes them?"

"The tree gets injured somehow, or maybe attacked by insects. I guess burls are like scabs, maybe? Anyway, they don't keep the tree from growing."

"You go, Mabel." I pat the rugged bark. "Is that why you like her? Because she keeps going, even when bad stuff happens to her?"

He rests his hand on the other side of the trunk. "I never thought about it that way, but maybe so." He leans there, looking up. Quiet. "Mostly, I like that she's always here."

My phone pings again. "Sorry," I say.

Where r u?

Ruffles.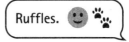

I add a smiley face and some paws to make up for falsely accusing her of spilling my secret.

Oh yeah. Forgot. Boring?

I glance at Emmett.

It's ok.

Call me when you get home. Found an awesome recipe!

k.

I repocket my phone. "I better get going."

"I know." He ducks his head. Embarrassed? "It's pathetic to like a tree. But she'll probably be here after we're—" He doesn't need to finish the sentence. Because I know. Most kids our age never give a thought to dying. He and I don't have that luxury anymore. Emmett starts pulling some weeds around the plaque. "Go on ahead. I'm going hang here for a while." Message between the lines: *I want to be by myself.* I totally get it.

Ruffles groans to a stand when I tug on her leash. "Thanks for the introduction," I tell him.

But what I really mean is, I wish we weren't members of the same club.

Chapter 11

On Monday, there's a new poster outside the cafeteria: FRIENDS ARE LIKE STARS. YOU CAN'T ALWAYS SEE THEM, BUT YOU KNOW THEY'RE ALWAYS THERE. Annoyingly sappy. But when I see Elly and Rajit making goofy faces at me from our table, I have to admit that poster may have a point. I crush Elly in a hug.

"What's this?" She's usually the hugger.

"Just happy to see you." I squeeze again and let go, so grateful to know I can really trust her with my secrets. Mrs. Medcalf, not so much.

"Look at this." Elly spreads the contents of her brown paper lunch sack on the table. PB&J. Cucumber rounds. Pear slices. "What's missing?" she asks.

"Is this one of those memory games?" Rajit sets his lunch tray on the floor.

"All the food pyramid basics." I peel the lid off a container of coconut yogurt, jealous of Elly's sandwich and Rajit's loaded baked potato, all of which are on my ever-longer "do-not-eat" list.

"Um. Dessert." She waggles her eyebrows. "You were supposed to do a practice bake yesterday."

"What are you, my boss?" I ask this with a smile.

"Is there something for me?" Rajit whimpers.

"You nut. Yes." I hand over waxed paper packages.

"Cookies?" Elly frowns. "What about that galette recipe I found? It's the middle of December! You've got to step up your game, girl. Five months till the big bakeroo." She sets the package aside. "Maybe I should make you a spreadsheet."

"Not cookies. Homemade Snickers bars."

"What? There's such a thing?" She tears into the bag, takes a bite. "Oh my gosh. So good. You are definitely going to win."

"Mooch alert!" Rajit hides his treat bag on his lap.

Dylan peers over Elly's shoulder. "That looks tasty."

She makes hamster noises as she answers, "Homemade Snickers." But she doesn't offer him one.

Dylan scans his lunch tray. "Trade you for a granola bar?"

"Puh-lease." Elly breaks off a piece. Pops it into her mouth. Makes nom-nom noises.

"Okay. Okay." He winces. "What if I listen to an entire album of your choosing?"

Elly puts a finger to her cheek. "Any album? Cross your heart?"

"If I do, I'll drop this." He lifts his lunch tray. "But I promise."

"Deal." She sets one of the squares next to his pizza slice. "I'll let you know in Student Council tomorrow which one I pick."

"I hope you like banjo music," Rajit warns.

"Or polkas," I add.

Dylan groans and heads off for his own table.

"It must not be true love if you aren't willing to share your dessert." I poke at my yogurt.

"*Homemade* Snickers." She nibbles a cucumber round. "'The course of true love never did run smooth.' Shakespeare."

"'Never get between a girl and her chocolate.' Rajit." He smirks.

"Ha ha." Elly throws a carrot at him.

Three days of coconut yogurt is two days too many. I scoot it aside. "You said there's a Student Council meeting tomorrow. Have you guys figured out a way to make the dance work?"

"That's what's on the agenda." Elly flips open her water bottle cap. "Everyone else is ready to give up. But not me. Not yet. It's our graduation dance!"

Emmett and Tenley wander by. "Hey. Can we get one of those things you gave Dylan?"

Elly covers her remaining candy square with her lunch sack. "Sorry. All gone."

"Ask Dylan to share," Rajit suggests.

"He ate it all. Right in front of us," says Emmett.

"So rude." Tenley plays with her newly purple-streaked hair.

"I'll bake something for tomorrow," Elly says.

"You?" Tenley coughs.

"Tenley." Emmett bounces on his toes, looking embarrassed.

Elly covers her face with her hands. "Okay. Okay. Tess is the star baker here."

"Figures." Emmett's cheeks dimple up when he smiles. "Ms. Bread Science."

"Runs in the family," I remind him. Tenley does not appreciate him talking to me. She grabs his hand and tugs him away.

"What he sees in her—" Elly doesn't finish her sentence.

"I told you." Rajit looks like he flunked a big test. "Now we are going to be swarmed by the moochers. Good thing you need lots of practice for the bake-off."

"I can't feed the entire eighth grade." I peel open a packet of saltines. Then I stop and grab Elly's arm.

"Elly." I stretch her name into about twelve syllables. "What do middle schoolers want more than anything?"

"Good grades?"

Rajit jumps in. "Lockers that open?"

"You guys!" I drop my head. "No. No. No. Sugar."

"Oh, right." Rajit points toward Emmett's table. "Case in point."

"What if we turn moochers into money?"

Blank stares.

I megaphone my hands around my mouth. "Two words: *bake sale.*"

Elly shrieks so loud the lunch ladies glare our way. "It's brilliant. We can make those great big cookies like they sell at the bakery and charge three bucks apiece for them."

"We?" Rajit interjects. "Does that include the girl who bakes cookies at 500 degrees?"

"Hey. I've had lessons from an expert." She points at me.

"One lesson," I clarify. "Anyway, don't you have to run the idea by the rest of the Student Council? And Mr. Gainor?"

"Trust me. The man lives for brownies. Sure, I'll have to present this to the council tomorrow. But I guarantee it's a done deal." She grabs me in a bone-crunching hug. "You are the best."

"Anything to help a friend," I say. And I mean it. Big-time.

Today's prompt in LA is: "One thing I learned from a significant adult in my life." There's a lot of groaning going on. "Annnd, the timer starts now," Mrs. Chatterjee says.

I spiral my pen over my journal, air writing, until a safe-enough memory comes. I'm still writing when the timer goes off.

Mrs. Chatterjee's given up on asking for volunteers. "Scholar Medina?" Lucky me. The first victim. Fabulous. I do a quick scan to see if I can get through what I wrote without my voice cracking. Seems doable. I take a deep breath and start.

"'My dad's bakery was right next door to a health foods store. Go figure, right? One Saturday, when I was helping, the owner went ballistic because of where a delivery truck parked. She screamed at Dad, but he didn't yell back. He asked the delivery guy to move down the block, then they carted the flour and stuff to the store. Afterward, Dad disappeared into the kitchen and emerged a couple hours later with a brand-new low-fat, low-sugar cookie. For the health food lady! I said, Why bother? And he said that you catch more flies with honey than with vinegar. She practically cried when he gave her the cookies and apologized for yelling about the truck. After that, he baked the healthy version every Saturday and called them Joyful Cookies, because the lady's name was Joy. She became his best customer. Especially on Saturdays.'" I finish reading and sit back down, fast, before any risky memories bubble up.

"Using honey rather than vinegar certainly is an important lesson. Thank you, Scholar Medina." Mrs. Chatterjee looks around the room. "Scholar Tanner?"

Brooklyn's chair protests as she stands, as if it knows what's coming. "This is kind of short," she says.

"Brevity is the soul of wit." Mrs. Chatterjee's bracelets tinkle as she motions for her to continue.

The look on Brooklyn's face sets my Spidey senses tingling.

"One thing I've learned from my LA teacher—"

I hold my breath.

"Is that kids don't count when it comes to their own education. The end."

Twenty-five heads twitch forward to catch Mrs. Chatterjee's reaction.

"To my ear, that did not sound like fifty words." Mrs. Chatterjee makes some kind of note in her grade book then calls on Tenley, as if nothing has happened. But Brooklyn walks out of class when the bell rings with a detention slip in her hand.

I catch her eye as she passes me in the hall.

"Honey." She tucks a braid behind an ear.

I shake my head. "I don't know if it'd help in this situation."

She sniffs. "You know what my grams says? Water wears away stone. I am water. I'll find a way."

"Maybe you should've written about your grams?" I suggest.

She waves the detention slip. "Now you tell me."

Chapter 12

Mom looks out the window. "I didn't realize the crew was coming over so early today."

"The video's due next week. January 31. Remember?" My Christmas gift to Mom had been coming clean about the bake-off. She took it pretty well, considering. But she made me pinky swear to get my LA grade up. I promised, even though I'm not sure I can deliver. Me getting a better grade from Mrs. Chatterjee is as likely as Elly getting macarons right on her first try.

"I was hoping we could chat before I head to the studio this morning."

My stomach flips at the way she says "chat."

Why did there have to be a teacher-parent portal? "I'm trying, Mom. I really am." I'd even had Elly help me with the last essay. Not even her honors fairy dust could save me. Another C minus.

"That's not what—" Mom's interrupted by Gracie's screeching.

"Elly! My Elly!" She flings herself through the front door.

Mom shakes her head. "To be continued."

"Hold up, munchkin!" Elly juggles the tripod; Wayne catches it before it crashes to the floor.

"What about us?" Rajit asks.

"You're my friends, too," Gracie reassures him. "And Rexi."

Rexi wags nose to tail at the sight of my sister, a literal treat machine.

Mom shrugs into her coat. "Have fun, you guys." She smooches Gracie good-bye and whisks out the door.

Rajit's calling out everyone's assignment.

"What should we do?" Gracie dances Mr. Monkey around.

"Can you babysit Rexi?" He takes the tripod from Wayne.

"It's a pretty big job, but I know you can manage it." Elly sheds her jacket and heads for the kitchen. Rajit follows.

Wayne hands Gracie a packet of treats. "Not too many, okay?"

"I'm going to teach her to high-five." Gracie plunks on the floor. "It's like shake only gooder."

"Awesome." Wayne picks up a duffle and heads for the kitchen, too. "Coming, Tess?"

At first, it had seemed like a good idea to have my friends help me with this competition video. But now I feel a little wobbly about an audience.

Elly turns off the overhead light. "Lighting from above is bad. Is there a lamp we can shine on you?"

"Where did you learn about lighting?" I ask.

"From the six YouTubes I watched. And the camera should be a couple inches above your sightline, not right at it."

"What about the lamp in the living room?" I suggest.

Wayne grabs it and sets it up on the kitchen counter. "How's this?"

Elly ratchets up the tripod, looking through my phone to check. "Perfect."

"Wait!" Rajit waves his hands. "How about makeup? I watched a TikTok."

"Maybe some blush and lip gloss?" Elly says, as if I'm not standing right there.

"I borrowed some of my cousin's stuff." Rajit holds up a retro makeup case.

I pull a lip gloss from my pocket and swipe it over my lips. "I'm good. Seriously."

Rajit looks disappointed. "Well then, what about a chef's coat?"

"Don't have one. It's okay. This is about the baking, not about me."

"All part of the package." He makes a frame with his hands like a film director. "An apron at least?"

"I should've just done this by myself."

"There is no 'I' in team," Elly pronounces. "Apron."

I rummage in the drawer, avoiding the white one with my name in red stitching. "Apron. Happy?"

Rajit makes a face. "It's a little busy. Do you have a plain one?"

"No." I tie it on.

"Okay. Okay. We'll work with it."

"I've created a monster. Several monsters." I look pointedly at Elly and Rajit.

"Not me." Wayne opens another bag and starts setting out snack food. "What are you baking?"

I gather up the ingredients and set them on the counter next to Bernice. "Ginger layer cake with poached pears and almonds with cream cheese frosting."

"Fancy!" Wayne crunches a tortilla chip.

"That's our girl." Elly turns her cap backward and peers through the phone's lens. "Ready?"

I scan the items on the counter. Something's missing. "Not yet."

Rajit helps himself to a handful of roasted almonds. The noisiest handful of nuts in history. I can't think with those Godzilla-sized nom-noms going on.

"Can you crunch quieter? Please?"

He covers his mouth. "Sorry."

"The ginger!" I scramble around the kitchen looking for the crystallized ginger.

"Is this it?" Wayne pulls a cellophane package out from under the chips bag.

I take it. "I hope I don't freak out like this at the bake-off."

"You won't." Rajit reaches for more almonds.

I clear my throat. "You are consuming essential ingredients."

He pushes the dish away. "Ready for action?"

Gracie runs in. "Look! She can do a high-five!"

"Do it again. I'll video you." Elly does and then Gracie watches the video. Three times.

This is going to take all day. "Hey, you know what? I bet Rexi would love to watch *PJ Masks*. Maybe Wayne could turn it on for you."

"It's her favorite," Wayne says. Gracie and Rexi tumble after him to the family room where he gets it all set up.

"She's good for at least an hour," I say.

"Then let's roll!" Rajit slaps his hands together.

In four. Out eight. "Now or never." I swipe my hands down the apron front.

Elly crouches down behind the phone. "Lighting looks really good. The apron's too wild, though. All those doughnuts."

"It was my birthday present from Gracie." I pick up a pear to end the discussion.

"Wait! I didn't get to say 'action' yet!" Rajit says.

I freeze.

"Action!"

"Thanks." I whisk the cider and spices in a pan.

"Shouldn't you be talking?"

"Should I?"

My question is answered by her snort.

"Okay. Hi. I'm Tess Medina. Today I'm baking ginger layer cake with poached pears and almonds with cream cheese icing. And, of course, I'm using my favorite product, Jubilee Flour."

"It doesn't have to be a commercial." Elly stands up.

"I can edit that out," Rajit says.

"Everyone's a critic." I definitely should've done this on my own.

She gets back behind the phone and Rajit makes a "roll camera" motion.

"Okay. Hi. I'm Tess Medina. Today I'm baking ginger layer cake with poached pears and almonds with cream cheese icing."

Elly gives a thumbs-up.

"While the pears poach, the oven's preheating to 320 degrees. Now it's time to start the cake." I grab the flour canister to start weighing.

"Cut!" Elly waves her hands around.

"What now?"

"I thought Tess was doing great." Wayne is the perfect cheerleader.

"She is. It's the apron." Elly shoves her cap back farther on her head. "Cuter than cute but not camera friendly. Don't you have anything less . . . wild?"

"Let me see." Rajit peers over her shoulder to watch the replay.

"Seriously?" I ask.

"Seriously," Rajit concurs.

"It's happy, with all those doughnuts, but kind of a lot," adds Wayne.

"I thought you were on my side." I loosen the ties. "Okay. Okay." Back to the drawer again. This time, I yank out Scott's BBQ apron, which only has a few tiny grease stains. "Happy now?"

She peeks through the phone. "Very. Take it from the top. That means start over from the beginning."

"I know." I reapply lip gloss and repeat the intro. When the cake layers go in the oven, we take a snack break. Elly shows us the video so far.

"I look goofy."

Wayne shakes his head. "Uhn-uh. You look baker-y."

"And confident," adds Rajit.

"Friends have to say nice things." I take a small sip of

water, hoping to wash away the prickles. That better not be the porcupine poking around.

"I am the kind of friend who would tell you if you looked goofy." Elly puts the phone back on the tripod. "And this is not goofy. It's"—she searches for a word—"earnest."

"Sounds as bad as goofy."

Elly tosses me two pot holders as the timer goes off. "Let me get you taking the layers out of the oven."

We take another break while the cakes cool before Elly and Rajit go all Steven Spielberg again while I whip up the cream cheese icing. Wayne wanders away to watch *PJ Masks* with Gracie. I slice the poached pears paper thin. Dad would be proud. Last step is to assemble and frost.

"Annnd that's a wrap." Elly stretches.

"Time for taste testing!" Rajit announces. That gets Gracie, Wayne, and Rexi's attention. I hand slices all around and hold my breath. Elly drapes herself dramatically over the counter. "This is the best thing I've ever put in my mouth."

"I didn't even think I liked pears." Rajit cuts another thin slice.

"Can I give Rexi a bite?" Gracie asks.

"A teeny, tiny one." Wayne licks his fingers. "You are going to win for sure."

"Aren't you having any?" Elly takes the knife from Rajit.

I poke my finger toward my mouth. "Too many practice bakes."

"More for us, then!" She cuts another slice.

"Save some for my folks."

"Okay, okay. Can I take a piece for Mom?"

We end up making up care packages for each of them to take home.

"I'll edit the video tonight," Rajit says. "It'll be ready to go tomorrow morning, first thing."

Elly gooshes me in a bear hug. "Best baker and plain old bestie."

"Thanks, you guys." I am absolutely drained. Maybe I need to start taking vitamins. "I couldn't do this without you."

"I was the biggest help, right, Elly?" Gracie asks.

"You better believe it!" Elly kisses her forehead.

"Team Tess!" Wayne pumps his fist as he hops down the steps.

Elly skips to her mom's car. "I come bearing gifts," she calls.

Mrs. Liu taps the horn and waves. "Our dentist is thrilled that you've come into our lives." She laughs then pulls away. Even though I'm shaky, I stand there until they're out of sight. I want to crawl in my bed, but I have to clean up the kitchen.

"Can I watch another show?" Gracie swipes her finger across the empty cake plate. "You are a real baker. Just like Dad."

Her words are a pinprick on my heart. "Thanks. Yeah. One more show." I set her up and head back to the kitchen.

There's one leftover egg on the counter. I hold it, cool and heavy, in my palm. All 57 grams of it. I know the weight because of Dad.

My pulse swishes in my ears; my vision blurs. How many grams are there in a memory? So many that my body can't stay upright. In my room, I grab Owlie from his hiding place and hug him close to shut everything out. But it doesn't work.

A stick of butter is 113 grams; a cup of flour, 120. There are 240 in a cup of milk.

The human heart weighs about 310 grams. That's what Pastor Katy said at the memorial. "A little over a half a pound. Picture two small bananas. A baby guinea pig. One running shoe. The human heart is such a small thing, really, about this big." She raised a closed fist. "Not measured by size or weight, but by actions." She held out a handful of envelopes. "These are a few of the letters Sarah's gotten. Here's one: 'Every couple months Tony opened his bakery to people like me. He got out the cloth napkins and real dishes and served us a fancy breakfast like we mattered. I must've eaten that breakfast four or five times before he asked me to help crack eggs. Next thing I knew, I had a job. And a place to live. All because of Tony.'" Pastor Katy read a thank-you from the food pantry Dad supported. A funny poem from a busboy about how Dad tried to convince him that ballet was a lot like football. A card from Joy at the health food store. People were crying and laughing, all at the same time. And the Tony stories didn't stop when the service was over.

I have so many of my own. Like, no matter how busy he got at the bakery, we had standing dates: Taco Tuesdays. Try-Something-New Thursdays. And every Sunday, when the bakery was closed, we took a long walk that ended up at Hilaria's Peruvian food truck. We'd eat lomo saltado and then hit up Mary's Dairy for ice cream—Cookie Dough for me, lemon sorbet for Dad.

I flop back on the bed, stare at the ceiling, and watch jerky old home videos roll by in my mind: Dad frosting cookies. Building sand wedding cakes on vacation at Birch Bay. Bedtime stories about a friendly monster called the Glibby-Glurb. Silly stuff. Baby stuff.

Stuff I miss big-time.

I pick up my phone.

I'm thinking about adding a pinch more ginger. Maybe candied, too? But I think you'd give my bake today a thumbs-up. I could def serve it to Chef Marie.

I hit send, then touch my ring, wishing for an answer.

My bedroom door opens. "I'm hungry." Gracie plops on my bed, Mr. Monkey tucked under her arm. "Why is your nose red?"

I pull her close. "It was itchy. How about tomato soup?"

"With toasted cheese?"

"You got it." I feel like crashing, not making lunch. But maybe this is my answer. Taking care of my sister is another way to keep Dad close. "Do you feel like watching the *British Baking Show*?"

"Yay!" She bounces off the bed and heads for the family room.

I follow. A Viennese swirl can cure anything.

Chapter 13

One rare, bright February morning, after I agree with Elly for the eightieth time that it's "epic" that the Student Council approved the idea of the bake sale, I grab my white-and-lime-green running shoes. I jog a few steps in place on the porch, letting the day's warmth wash over me. Solar powered inside and out, I head to Mr. Jackson's, debating what to make my friends for Valentine's Day. Kind of leaning toward chocolate-covered strawberry cupcakes even though I really want to do lava cakes. But there's no way to serve them hot at school. I chat about the weather for a minute with Mr. Jackson before Ruffles and I head out. My ears fill up with "Gonna Run" and I lean into the rhythm of the music, lean into the rhythm of my body. It takes Ruffles a half a block to figure out what we're doing, but after I give her a chance to bark at a couple of squirrels, she gets on board. The solid thumping of my two feet and her four paws creates a sassy beat and I lean into that, too.

My feet push against the solid earth, borrowing energy from the depths. With my brain pumping out endorphins, I'm so chill, I wave a car to go ahead even though I'm in the crosswalk. When I hit the curb on the other side, I pick up the pace and Ruffles matches me, lumbering into higher gear.

Six legs pump past now familiar landmarks. The Tabers' house on the right, the Baptist church up on the corner. Today their reader board says, IF SPEAKING KINDLY TO PLANTS CAN MAKE THEM GROW, IMAGINE WHAT SPEAKING KINDLY TO HUMANS CAN DO. Miss Patti's Daycare, a couple streets over, takes up half the block. *Plod, swish, plod, swish.* By the time I hit the middle of the playlist, we're at Carlyon Park.

"Once around?" My fluffy black companion shakes herself, tail to nose, and I'm baptized by slobber. I take that as a yes. We make an easy loop past the play structure and the tennis courts, then follow the trail into the woods to say hi to Mabel; she seems glad for the company. Ruffles studies a squirrel chattering at her from the safety of a nearby cottonwood. The air shimmers with birdsong and whispering birches. I lean up for a glimpse of Mabel's top branches. Is she done growing or will those needled arms someday snag a star or two? My gaze travels down to that burl. I thought it was ugly when Emmett first pointed it out, but now it looks like a work of art. Rich brown and whorled like a fingerprint or a cowlick. I've heard people say tree hugging is for nature nuts, but I don't agree. We could all learn something from trees. About standing tall and calm, no matter what happens. I think Emmett would like it that

I came to visit Mabel on my own. Maybe I'll tell him. When Tenley's not around.

Ruffles harrumphs; the squirrel's moved on and she's bored. "Ready to head back?" As I give Mabel one last pat, I notice a huge maple leaf, half-green and half-butter yellow. I pick it up because it has Gracie art project written all over it.

By the time we pop out of the trees, the sun has ducked behind a cloud and the temperature drops—bam—along with my energy. Like a trap door's opened and it's gone. Maybe I shouldn't have pushed it. Walked more of the route. Please don't let that be the porcupine.

I collapse on a bench, breathing hard, twirling Gracie's leaf. Ruffles's tongue is a pink yo-yo bobbing in and out. She sniffs my right shoe, then circles three times before resting her blocky head on my lap. I weave my fingers through her warm soft fur, which helps slow my breath. *In four. Out eight.* Maybe I can stop the porcupine by going to my happy place. Focus on baking. And those pears Mom bought at the farmers' market. My go-to blogger recently posted a recipe for a pear clafoutis. I don't know how to pronounce it, but the photos make it look delicious.

My body temp drops again, turning my vertebrae into ice cubes. I can't stop shivering. "Let's go, big girl." Ruffles doesn't move. I get it. I don't want to, either. But I have to get home. Get warm. Stop shaking. I've dropped Gracie's leaf somewhere, but I can't go back. Only forward.

"Come on, Ruff." Something scrapes inside as I ease into a jog. The pain makes me stumble; Ruffles breaks my fall. This is no porcupine. My body senses danger, and tries to turn inside out to expel this anomaly, this foreign object. This Knife. I have to stop. And I have to keep moving. Home. Let me get home.

The Knife clicks through all twenty Swiss Army options until the biggest blade snaps into place. Dread and a vile liquid, both bitter, rise up my throat. No. No! What was I thinking? I never should have run toward the park. It's probably the last five-mile stretch in the entire world without a lovely clean Starbucks bathroom.

In four. Out eight.

Waiting is not an option.

Miss Patti's Daycare is dead ahead.

I limp onto the porch and wrap Ruffles's leash around the bright yellow railing. I'm writhing now, clenching my butt cheeks. I have to get in. *Knock, knock, knock.* Nothing. Can she hear me over all the kid noise? I pound. Try not to cry. After an eternity, a woman with a flowered apron cracks the door. "I'm busy right now." Clearly ticked off that I'm on her porch.

"Sorry to bother you, but could I use your bathroom?" I can't stand up straight, can't look her in the eyes as I ask. Beg. The blade slices deeper. I stifle a gasp.

"This is a private business."

Tears pull at my eyes. "I know, I am so sorry." *Please. Please.* "It's an emergency." *Please.*

She starts to open her mouth. She's going to say no. Then what?

"Okay, fine, but make it quick." Maybe she reads the sheer panic on my face. She probably deals all day with kids who have to go. Now.

The toilet is tiny, installed at the proper height for a three-year-old. I don't care. Nothing has looked more beautiful in my life.

I wash trembling hands in the kid-sized sink, splotchy with finger paint and remnants of old stickers. My mirrored reflection is surrounded by safari animals. Relief gives way to shame. What a loser. Reduced to pounding on strangers' doors, begging to use the bathroom. I catch cold water in my cupped hands and take a couple sips. The water bounces at the bottom of my stomach, it's that empty. And so sore from the Knife's twisting and turning. And I still have to get myself and Ruffles home. It's too much. I turn away from the mirror to keep from bawling. Then I sneak out the front door, my arms noodles as I untie Ruffles's leash. She's gotten comfy on the porch; her huge yawn shows black patches on the pink roof of her mouth.

"Come on, Ruff. Help me out here." With a grunt she

scrambles to her feet as I tug. Finally, she gets with the program and we're off, her lumbering along at my heels. I lumber along, too, on legs made of petrified wood. It takes all my will to pick them up. Put them down again.

I had no idea humiliation could be so heavy.

Chapter 14

"Are you still up for helping me at the studio today?" Mom frowns. "You look kind of peaked."

That's her word for sick. And I am. Have been all week since the Miss Patti's horror story. But mostly with embarrassment. "Cramps," I say. Just not the kind she thinks. "I'll be ready as soon as I brush my teeth."

"Maybe take a break from that Titan Power sweatshirt?" She brushes my hair back from my face. "I'm all for school spirit, but it's not your best look."

I change to a white tee and my darkest jeans, which kind of matches Mom's work outfit of white blouse and black jeans.

Gracie needs about five more kisses before we leave. "Honey, I'll be late. Gotta go!" Mom grabs her gear, and we fly out the door and down the road. I peek at the speedometer. Dad said five over wasn't speeding. Mom's definitely speeding. Hopefully, Scott will teach me to drive.

The whole day is a rush of setting up fills, light umbrellas, wrangling clients. There's barely time to eat the hummus wraps Mom packed for lunch. Now also on the do-not-eat list.

When the last client is out the door, Mom collapses on the couch. If she hadn't beat me to it, I would've, too. Even my teeth are tired.

"You were a saint. Especially with the dog family." She'd finally gotten two moms, two kids, and two dogs arranged just the way she wanted them when the littlest dog let loose a stream of pee that beat anything Ruffles produces. Of course, the dog walker got stuck with cleanup.

"I think you got some good shots."

She stretches. "Wasn't that fiftieth-anniversary couple adorable?"

"She was my age when they met."

"Yeah, well. Different times." Mom pinches the bridge of her nose. "I always thought your dad and I would get our fifty years."

I plunk on the couch next to her. "Me too."

She sniffles. "God, I miss him."

I lean close, wrapped in her pear-and-freesia scent. I've never been but she smells like Paris. And love. "Me too. Sometimes, I think he's helping with the competition. I mean, that pear cake was—"

"Sophisticated. Fantastic. Super delicious." She laughs. "Let me know when to stop."

"You forgot scrummy."

"And that. He'd be proud of you whether you make it to the next level or not." She leans her head against mine.

"However, he wouldn't be so yippy-skippy about your LA grade."

"I'm trying!" I'd even watched a whole series of YouTubes on writing essays. And still my latest essay got a purple C plus.

"Maybe you should try talking to Mrs. Chatterjee? Directly? Hear it from the horse's mouth?"

"Ugh."

"I say give it a shot." This is more command than suggestion.

"Okay. Okay." I push myself up off the couch.

"Hey. Don't move!" Mom swings up her camera and clicks away. Checks the images and makes a face I can't decipher. "Look at this." She scrolls through pictures. "This was at Scott's birthday. In July. And this is today." Mom toggles back and forth between the two photos. "Do you see the difference?"

"No."

"You've lost weight." Her voice is sad.

"I don't think so." But my jeans are looser. "Anyway, the scale disappeared in the move, remember?" Mom doesn't play along with my attempted joke. "It's not like I'm anorexic or anything."

"I don't know." Mom stuffs the camera in her bag. Looks straight at me. "Are you?"

"No." I'd be happy to eat more. It's the Knife that stops me. "If I were, would I be doing all that baking?"

"I truly don't know." She wraps her hair into a messy bun then lets it fall. "I think we should get it checked out."

"We?"

She rests her hand on my shoulder. "You."

"There's nothing. Seriously." I shake her off. "I don't need to go to the doctor."

"Well, I need you to." She zips up the camera bag. "Or no bake-off."

"Mom!"

"That's final." She switches off the light and opens the door.

My phone pings.

How's it going?

Elly must be home from her aunt's birthday party.

I type a reply.

Just peachy.

Then I follow Mom to the car.

I take Mom's suggestion and stay after on Monday to talk to Mrs. Chatterjee about my grade. "No matter what you write, I come away wondering where Tess Medina is in this piece of work," Mrs. Chatterjee says. "Sometimes it helps a writer to dictate to herself; that can be a wonderful springboard into writing. Or have you tried using a graphic organizer?"

She pulls a couple organizers out of a tidy file cabinet and hands them over like she's giving me a triple-chocolate brownie instead of work. Organization is not my problem. I'll just never, ever, ever understand how to write. At least not the way Mrs. Chatterjee wants me to. And Mom's not mean, but school comes first to her. If I don't pull up this grade, she really will put her foot down about the bake-off. Not getting to compete is as painful as the Knife, which has hardly given me a break lately.

It's turned me into an expert on locating public restrooms. There is one women's room, five stalls with very short doors, at the library where we take Gracie for story time. Mom's favorite mall has a Target—one bathroom, immediately to the left of the main entrance—and two Starbucks. One of them requires a security code for the bathroom; luckily, Mom's favorite barista works at the other one. We grocery shop at QFC—bathroom at the back, near the wine department—and Haggen—past the produce, through a swinging door. At school, there are three girls' bathrooms, one on each floor. And, of course, three for teachers, but I'd get busted using those. I've developed mad tracking skills; I'm surprised the FBI hasn't tried to recruit me.

I slip the organizers into my pack and thank Mrs.

Chatterjee even though I feel anything but thankful. It's a long walk home.

"Hey, Tess—" Mom catches me on my way to my room. "Is something up?"

I turn my head so she can't see the tear trickling down my cheek.

"You okay?" She puts her arm around my waist. Tugs. "Was it the talk with Mrs. Chatterjee?"

"Sort of. She gave me some organizers. But I don't feel very good." I press my tender abdomen. "I don't know. My breakfast smoothie didn't agree with me."

"What's that mean? Nausea? Diarrhea?"

"I guess both. Maybe I'm developing a dairy allergy?" I want to tell her about everything. The mile-long do-not-eat list. The clean undies stashed in my backpack just in case since the Miss Patti's thing. But I don't want to mess up my chance to go to the bake-off. And it really could be that I've developed an intolerance.

She steps back to look me over. "How long has dairy been bugging you?"

I shrug. "A while."

She pulls me close again. "I'll pick up some lactose-free milk. And some, I don't know, almond milk yogurt." She grabs a pencil and makes a note on the grocery list. "In the meantime, let's get you to a doctor. I've been meaning to set us all up at a new clinic. I'm sorry."

"You've had work. And stuff. It's okay. Really."

"Do you want some Pepto?" She ducks into her bathroom and comes out with a bottle of pink liquid. She squints to read the label. "Start with two tablespoons every thirty to sixty minutes."

I gag thinking about swallowing the pink guck. But maybe it will help. "Was there something you wanted? When I came in?"

"You got a letter. It's on the kitchen counter."

"A letter?" I hand back the Pepto. "Or *the* letter?"

She squeezes my shoulder. "Better see for yourself."

I don't know if I can handle bad news today. But I also can't handle not knowing. Best to rip off the Band-Aid. I slit the envelope and ease the letter out, squinting. Bold type catches my eye: **Congratulations!**

I scream. "I did it!"

Gracie tackles me. "You won! You won!"

I lean against the counter, processing the news. Wait till I tell Elly! "Not quite."

"Not yet, you mean." Mom smiles.

"There's another step before the bake-off." I skim through the letter. "Have you ever heard of TeaTime Bakery? I have to bake something for the owner to judge."

Mom gets her phone out and googles. "Downtown Bothell. Not too far."

"My sister is the best baker ever!" Gracie bounces in circles. "Woo-hoo!"

I leave them planning my celebration dinner and call Elly. She squeals and immediately orders a Saturday sleepover.

"I can't, El. Uh, I'm helping Mom at the studio on Sunday. Early." Elly's habit of chatting into the wee hours isn't a problem; last time I slept over, I zonked out for a while, and when I woke up, she was still talking. Hadn't even noticed I'd been asleep. The problem is her bathroom, or rather, its location right off her bedroom. And it would be weird to go down the hall to use the other one. Maybe when my stomach's better.

"What if I promise not to talk all night? Lights out at eleven?" Elly manages to make puppy dog eyes with her voice. "Ten thirty? We've got to party! You made it through the first round."

"I can't. Really. Also have to rewrite that essay for Chatterjee."

Heavy sigh in my ear. "Well, can I come over after you get back from helping your mom? Two minds are better than one when it comes to deciding what to make for that baker."

"That would probably work out. I'll text you when I get home."

"I'm thinking macarons. Or éclairs. Or maybe a galette." Her voice brightens; nothing she loves more than a project. At least it's not germs.

"Great ideas. More later. Gotta go." I really did.

We decide on éclairs. When I say "we," I mean Elly. She watched a bunch of kids' baking shows and by some mysterious calculation proclaimed éclairs the best way to get a judge's attention. "And you gotta *dip* them in the chocolate glaze." She mimes dipping as we head to TeaTime Bakery. "Not spread it on."

"Or cinnamon glaze, which is what I'm making to go with the maple pastry cream."

"Cinnamon. Chocolate." She flaps her hands around. "Whatever. Dip."

Scott glances over his shoulder. "You sure you don't want me to come in? Mrs. Medcalf said she'd keep Gracie as long as we need her to."

"One chaperone is enough," I say. And actually one person may be too many, given that it's Elly. But she is my self-appointed life coach and cheerleader. And she somehow managed to explain things to Rajit and Wayne so they didn't feel left out.

"There it is." Scott eases into a parking spot a few doors down from the bakery.

"I need Pepto." I pretend like I'm making a joke, but I'm

for real. My stomach's doing gymnastics. Nerves, though. Not the Knife.

"You've got this." Elly opens the car door. "Be ready to throw the confetti when we're through here, Scott."

He salutes. "Aye-aye, Captain."

Elly pushes through the door like she owns the place. "Is Marla Garrity here?"

I juggle my grocery sack of ingredients to catch the door so it doesn't slam shut. The jingling bell reminds me of Tony's. Of Dad. I inhale. No Doublemint but plenty of yeast.

A frizzy-haired lady with heart-shaped red glasses pops her head over the display case. "That's me! Are you Tess?"

Elly points. "She is. I'm moral support."

"Welcome, Moral Support." Marla's laugh is warm and rich like caramel sauce. "I promise not to be too harsh. Come this way, ladies, and I'll show you where to set up."

The rules are that I have to use TeaTime's equipment, but I tucked Dad's éclair stencil in my pocket just in case. Eyeballing four and a half inches—the perfect éclair standard—is not for the faint of heart. I see that Marla's got one on the counter with the other supplies. Still, having Dad's is a comfort. Like when I went to kindergarten and Mom snipped off a tiny bit of Owlie's scarf for me to keep in my pocket. It got me through that first week, that's for sure.

Marla reads the rules aloud, then supervises as I set each ingredient on the counter. "No chocolate?" Her darkened eyebrows float above her glasses. My heart sinks a little. Maybe I should've gone for the traditional.

"You will not be disappointed," Elly promises. Marla smiles noncommittally.

"I think I have to start timing you as soon as you get everything set out. Need a bathroom break first? It's right through there." Marla points.

Do I? Gut check. Everything seems quiet aside from the tsunami of nerves sloshing around in my stomach. "I'm okay."

Elly plops a water bottle on the counter. "Stay hydrated. Can I sit over here?" She moves toward a rickety wooden chair.

Marla nods. "Setting the timer for two hours. Ready. Bake!"

The first egg I crack totally misses the bowl, and I waste a couple precious minutes cleaning that up. Precious minutes because the fastest I've been able to whip up this recipe is one hour and forty-five minutes. No more mistakes. Luckily, I can make choux pastry in my sleep; that comes together smoothly and I stick it in Marla's fridge to cool. I preheat the oven to 400 degrees, then prep my baking sheets by covering them with parchment paper misted with water. Important step because all those eggs need moisture. I pipe out the choux dough with the French star tip and make sure they are all exactly the same magic length. Twenty minutes at 400 degrees then I'll crank the temp down to 350. But no peeking because you can absolutely under no circumstances open the oven door or you'll have éclair pancakes.

Time to start the maple pastry cream. The trickiest part is tempering the eggs as you add them to the warm milk. Just a spoonful at a time.

"Timer!" Elly calls.

I set the cream aside and run to the oven.

"Ahem." Marla clears her throat. "No coaching."

Elly covers her mouth. "Sorry. Nerves."

I lower the oven temp and reset the timer for ten minutes. I work the pastry cream through a sieve so it's lusciously smooth and check on the éclairs. Not quite browned enough. After a couple more minutes, I set them on racks to cool.

Elly sniffs loudly. "Yum!"

Marla gives her a look.

Elly scrunches down on the chair. "Not another peep. I promise."

I could slice the cooled éclairs open, but I need to impress. So I take another tip and poke a couple holes in the bottom of each one so I can pipe in the maple pastry cream. The trick is filling every bit of the éclair, but I'm a pro, thanks to Dad. "Time?" I ask.

Elly leans forward as if to answer but catches herself.

"Fifteen minutes," Marla answers.

Okay. Bringing out the secret weapon then. I whip up the glaze and dip each éclair in the gooey cinnamon goodness. Then I grab a small sauté pan, melt some sugar, water, and salt together, and toss in a handful of chopped pecans. I don't have enough time to let them cool, but Marla's got a blast chiller and it does the trick. With a minute to go, I decorate my pastries with the crystallized nuts.

"Time!" Marla calls. I step away from the serving platter, and Elly flings herself at me.

"You did it! And they're gorgeous." She turns to Marla. "Aren't they?"

Marla's face gives nothing away. "Nicely plated," she says.

I take a few nervous sips of water as she tastes one, making notes. "Are you allowed to tell me anything?"

"Sorry. No." Marla points to a stack of pastry boxes. "You can pack up the extras to take home."

I do that while Elly texts Scott to come get us.

"How'd it go?" he asks.

"Tess was a pro. But no idea what Marla thought." Elly opens the box, pulls out an éclair, and opens her mouth. "I hope you don't lose points because of me."

I catch Scott's eyes in the rearview mirror. "I actually think she liked them. A lot."

"This is—holy moly." Elly keeps talking with éclair in

her mouth. "Who wouldn't love these? But how do you know Marla does?"

I take a swig of water. "I made a dozen, but there were only ten to pack up. You don't eat two if you don't like them."

Elly squeals. "Portland, here we come!"

Chapter 15

Elly, Rajit, and Wayne meet us in the drop-off lane with two empty media carts. "You are not going to believe this." Elly grabs a box of cookies from Scott's trunk.

"The bake sale's cancelled?" I pop the lid on my water bottle. Oatmeal was clearly a bad breakfast choice.

She huffs. "No. Way more important."

"Than cookies?" Rajit stacks another box on his cart.

"Or cupcakes?" adds Wayne.

"Yes. Did you know that one of the people who helped to discover DNA was a woman? Have you ever heard of her? No! It's always Watson and Crick, Watson and Crick. But without Rosalind Franklin, those two never would've figured it out."

The Knife is clearly not a hot cereal fan. A razor wire hamster wheel rolls around my stomach. "Uh-huh." Breathe. Breathe. All I can manage is that *uh-huh*.

"I mean, she invented the X-ray camera so they could photograph it and she DIED from the radiation exposure." Elly pokes her head into the trunk. "Looks like that's the last. Thanks, Scott."

"Yeah, thanks," Rajit adds.

Scott gives me a hug. Then frowns. "You okay?"

In four. Out eight.

"A little tired." That part was true. Supervising yesterday's bake-a-thon with Elly, Rajit, and Wayne had been harder than walking Ruffles, Peanut, and Trixie all at the same time. You know that saying, "Not my circus, not my monkeys"? They were all my monkeys. I swear I swept up a couple cups of flour from the floor after they left. I hug Scott once more. "See you tonight."

The other three barrel inside with the cookies and I hustle to keep up. But I'm slogging through quicksand. And there are window blinds in my eyes flipping open and shut. The poster-covered walls swim and blur. Kids bump around and into me, spawning salmon rushing to their lockers before school. The nurse's door across the hall is ajar, framing a white-sheeted cot, cool and inviting. I could lie down. For a few precious minutes. Or maybe for the rest of my life.

"Tess?" Elly turns back. "What the heck? We've got a bake sale to set up."

"Uh, just processing that information. About the DNA lady?" Over Elly's shoulder, the nurse's cot sends out laser beams, luring me closer.

"Come on, slowpoke," Wayne calls.

I paste on a smile to match his, struggling through thickening quicksand. The Student Council peeps have tables set up in the main hallway. Wayne joins a couple tall kids on step stools, hanging VALENTINE'S DAY BAKE SALE posters behind the tables. Mr. Gainor sets out a cash box.

In a minute, the hall's a scene from a zombie movie, only instead of seeking brains, kids are seeking cookies. Brooklyn can't even get the cash box open before people start throwing money at her. Elly uses her drama voice: "Make your choice then pay over here. Make your choice then pay over here."

Three choir girls donate Rice Krispies Treats. A couple skater kids drop off a dozen baggies of Nuts and Bolts. Elly finds a place for each new donation while I slip on lunch lady gloves and do my best to ignore the Knife.

Wayne's next in line. "I'll take two of the oatmeal chocolate chips." He turns to the guy behind him. "I baked those."

The kid nods. "Cool. Can I have two of the same and one of the cupcakes?"

I fill his order along with Wayne's, while Elly collects the money. "Thanks for supporting the cause!"

"The cause?" the kid asks.

Elly points to the banner behind the table. "We're raising money for the graduation dance."

"Thought it got cancelled." The kid peels the paper from his cupcake as he wanders away. "Oh, hey, Dylan."

Dylan towers over the table. "Which ones did you make, Elly?"

She makes that squeaky hamster sound. Then she waves her hand over the whole cookie display. I raise an eyebrow. "Technically," she whispers.

Dylan holds out a twenty-dollar bill. "I'll take one of each. Those cupcakes look good, too. Did you bake those?"

Elly clears her throat. "Tess did."

"Even if Elly didn't bake them, you'll probably be able to gag one down." Rajit inserts himself into the conversation.

Dylan points a finger at Rajit. "Most definitely."

I hand over the full bakery bag. Elly takes Dylan's money. "Thanks for supporting the cause."

"Hope it earns me a dance with you!"

Elly answers in hamsterese.

"I'm pretty sure that means yes," Rajit interprets.

Red-faced, Elly turns to the next person in line. "What can I get you?"

"Where should I put these?" Emmett holds out a tray of buttercream-frosted cupcakes sprinkled with blue and green, our school colors.

"Those look professional!" I say. And they do. My stomach flutters. Oh my frog! Am I crushing on Emmett? We do have a lot in common. Our dads. Baking. But: Tenley. "I'll just put them—uh." Something bursts and my gut's bubbling like a disgusting prehistoric swamp. Gotta get out of here. I peel off my gloves. The nearest bathroom is on the second floor. Second floor! "Sorry. Be right back."

I'm halfway up the stairs when a horror film unspools in my innards. I double over, and kids swerve around, but no one yells at me. Another step, and the pain rolls me into a ball, sweat trickling down my sides. Maybe it wouldn't be so bad to go bumping down all these hard tile steps. Smash my head open. End all this.

"Drop something?" A kind voice enters my left ear. I shake my head and the speaker moves on.

The second floor might as well be Mount Rainier. I'm crab walking, but I don't even care. All that matters is reaching the bathroom before . . . no, don't even think about that. Hold it in. A few more steps.

The door handle is cool under my sweat-slick hand. I burst inside.

Some seventh grader is sprawled across the sink, slathering on black lipstick. This is the worst. When there's only one other person in the bathroom. No noise to hide behind. And I need to hide. No one wants to listen to me. Smell me. I sure don't. The girl leans back from the mirror, admiring her artwork. Pulls her phone from her pocket and snaps a selfie. The Knife buries itself too deep to stand upright.

"There's no paper in the first stall," she says.

I grit my teeth. "Thanks." Drag myself behind the second door. The seat is cold. I shut my eyes tight, praying the bathroom door will close.

It does. And my body turns into an angry volcano

spewing hot diarrhea. I hold my head and rock, overwhelmed by the pain and the stink. I can't do this anymore. My guts try to come out, to break free. Right now, I would be okay with that. Anything to stop the pain.

Forever passes before I can stand up, weaving like Gracie's Noodley Men. The pain worms its way deep into my bones, making itself at home, a deep bruise that can't heal. It's never going away. To keep from crying, I wash my face as well as my hands. Dry everything with a scratchy paper towel. I've got to get myself together to go back to the bake sale. Elly will be wondering.

Before I make it to the door, the Knife plunges deep. I grope for the wall, sliding down, down, down to a primordial ooze of germs. Disgusting as the floor is, I may never get up.

My head falls on pulled-up knees. A mix of tears and snot rubs off on the denim. I can't keep going like this. I can't.

The Knife is merciless, stabbing again and again. I drag myself from the filthy floor back to the stall.

This time, as I exit, the restroom door opens.

A dark head with deep green stripes.

"Tess?"

That's the last thing I hear.

Chapter 16

Unicorns.

Rainbow unicorns dancing on a navy-blue background. I blink a couple times to figure out if this is a dream or a nightmare.

"Well, there she is." A face sharpens into focus. A name tag. *Alix*. "Your parents went for coffee. They'll be right back." Her smile is friendly and there's kind of a music in her way of speaking.

I smack my lips. So dry. "Can I—" Do I even remember how to talk? "Can I have some water?"

"Of course." She hands me a refillable water bottle from a narrow bedside table. "You were pretty dehydrated."

My arm gets tangled up in tubing.

"We put in an IV," Alix explains. "To get some fluids in you. I'm sorry I can't bring you anything to eat."

"That's okay." My stomach's quiet, the Knife back in its sheath. No sense providing any ammunition.

"The doctor will be in soon to explain everything." She pulls a tall beeping machine over by the bed. "I need to get your vitals. Blood pressure and such."

"Am I okay?"

She pauses in her bustling. Holds my eyes with hers. "You are very sick, but the doctors will help you."

"I'm not going to die?"

"Oh, child." Now she's stroking my hand. I can't stop the tears rolling down my face, faster and faster. "You are *not* going to die." The stroking stops and she hands me a Kleenex. "At least, not until you are a very old woman with dozens of grandchildren and a bald, happy husband."

I wipe my face. "Does he have to be bald?"

"What's so funny?" Mom's at my side in two steps, brushing my hair back from my forehead. Scott stays at the end of the bed, rubbing my feet under the thin coverings.

"Tess questions my ability to predict her future." Alix winks and rolls the blood pressure machine away. "If you need anything, push that call button, right there." She shows me a remote attached to a white cord tucked at my side.

Mom presses her head to mine and I inhale her perfume, the coffee she drank. And more. Safety. Comfort.

In four. Out eight. "Where's Gracie?"

"With the Medcalfs. She'd probably be climbing all over you right now, wanting you to play Prairie or Little People or Dance Party." Mom sits back. "Not the best thing for the patient in need of rest."

"What's going on? Why am I here?"

"Do you remember fainting at school?"

Scott pulls up a chair and Mom sits. She reaches for my hand, but it's the one with the IV. She pats my leg instead.

Bits of blurry images float around in my memory. "Sort of." Ugh. The bathroom floor. I'll have to burn those jeans.

"Thankfully, that girl—Tenley—happened to be there. She caught you. Otherwise, you'd likely have a broken nose or concussion to go along with everything else."

Tenley. "What 'everything else'?" I ask.

Pat-pat on the leg. "Well, that's what the doctors want to figure out." *Pat-pat-pat.* "They have to do additional tests first."

"What kind of tests?"

Mom glances over at Scott, like she hopes he'll chime in. He doesn't. "They need to take a look at your stomach and intestines."

I pull my blanket up to my chin. "Gross."

"Not gross." A woman sweeps into the room, laptop under her arm, her white coat so crisply starched it looks like it could stand up on its own. "Fascinating." She holds out her hand. "I'm Dr. Lee. Oh, don't get up," she tells Mom. "I'll make myself at home right over here." She pulls up a chair on my other side, opens her laptop, and turns it so I can see. "We doctors are crazy about numbers and percentages and anything we can measure. Your blood work's off—sed rate up, iron down. Clearly, you are one sick girl." She pauses. "Young woman. Sorry. I have some suspicions about what's making you sick. But I need more information. Can I ask you a few questions?"

My phone pings. I can't help looking. Elly.

U fainted at school!

Dr. Lee's eyes follow mine. "Do you need to answer that?"

I slide the phone under my pillowcase. "Later," I say.

She leans forward. "You seem to have abdominal tenderness. Are your bowel movements normal? Any blood or mucus?"

She doesn't exactly pull punches. "No. Yes." I want to pull the sheet over my head.

She types. Nods. Types some more. "As I said, I need additional information. That means an endoscopy and a colonoscopy, which I've managed to schedule for tomorrow. So, I'm sorry, no burgers or ice cream or anything to eat until those are completed."

"That's okay. I'm not hungry anyway." Even the mention of food starts the Knife scratching at my insides.

"I'm betting you're not hungry because when you eat, your gut goes on a rampage. Is that right?"

I give a tiny nod.

"She's been losing weight," Mom adds.

"Not surprising. I mean, I wouldn't want to eat either if it meant running for a bathroom every ten minutes."

"It isn't quite that bad." My phone pings again. I fluff the pillow to cover up the noise.

Dr. Lee smiles. "You're a tough cookie, Tess. I can tell that. But no more suffering in silence. You and I are now a team. Your job is to do what you need to do to get better, and my job is to help you out when this—" She pauses as if searching for a word.

"Knife." I smooth the sheets over my stomach. "I call it the Knife."

Dr. Lee nods. "Apt description."

"Do you know what it is?" Scott asks.

A little waggle of the head. "As I said, I have a hunch, but let's get the test results back and we'll go from there." She closes the laptop. "What are your questions for me?"

It's all happening so fast I can't think of any. Maybe one. "Will they hurt? The tests?"

She wrinkles her nose. "The prep's no fun. You have to drink stuff that cleans you out. Big-time. I'm not going to pretend it tastes good. But for the tests, you, my friend, won't feel a thing, thanks to the miracles of modern medicine. You'll be sedated and sleep right through it all. Afterward, your throat might be sore from the scoping. Mom? Dad? Any questions from you?"

They shake their heads. "Not now, anyway," Scott says.

"Okay then." She pats the bed railing. "Now I'll leave you alone so you can text your friends."

But I don't.

"We need to relieve the Medcalfs. I know Gracie's worn them out," Mom says. "I'll be back after dinner."

"Don't rush." I shuffle my legs under the crisp sheets. "I'll probably sleep." The pillow buzzes again.

"You want us to call Elly?" Scott squeezes my hand.

"No!" I squeeze back. Let go. "I mean. No. I'll call her. Later."

Mom brushes her lips against my forehead. "We love you, honey."

I'm dozing when Alix bustles in to check my vitals. She refills my water bottle.

"Doing a good job with those fluids," she says. "Anything else I can get you? Do for you?"

As if on cue, my phone pings again.

She winds tubing around the blood pressure cuff and hangs it on the stand. "I'll give you some privacy."

She closes the door, blocking out all the hall noises. It's too quiet. I think about looking around for my earbuds, but most of my playlists are Elly-inspired. Can't go there right now.

> Hey. I bet you already know where I am. I'm guessing people don't faint because they're lactose intolerant, right? Whatever's wrong with me must be kinda bad. Lots of crummy stuff's been happening.

I stop for a second. That's true. But some good things have happened, too. Like Miss Patti letting me in. And the dog-walking jobs. And remembering that Chef Marie likes macarons. And all the times I caught a whiff of Doublemint.

I think you've been watching over me. Can you please keep it up?

I toss the phone aside, rub my salty wet face on the pillow, and pretend I'm snuggling Owlie.

Dr. Lee is honest, at least. The stuff I drink is beyond nasty. But, with Alix's cheerleading, I get it down.

She steps into the hall and waves in a gurney. "Your limo has arrived." She and Mom help me out of the bed and onto my ride. Mom walks next to it through the halls, going with me as far as they'll let her. It's kind of embarrassing and yet, when those double doors close, shutting her out and me in, I want to throw a Gracie tantrum and cry for Mommy. *In four. Out eight.* Doesn't help. My heart races as I lie there, alone. It's cold. Really cold. Teeth-chattering cold.

"I know it's chilly, but you won't be here too long." A nurse adjusts me on the gurney. "They'll bring you all the heated blankets you want in recovery."

Dr. Lee says hello, then another doctor steps to my side, his face hidden by a surgical mask. "Ready for a little nap?"

Then he tells me to count backward from ten and breathe deeply. Ten, nine, eight . . .

That nurse was right. They bring me all the blankets I want. And they always lift off the cooled one to put the fresh warm one right next to my body. Still, I can't seem to stop shivering.

"'The Princess and the Pea,'" Dr. Lee observes when she sees the mountain of blankets. "But she was on top, right?" Her brow wrinkles, trying to remember.

"Mattresses," I say.

"Oh, yeah. That's right." She nods. "My oldest son loved that story. I had to read it every night when he was around four. I should remember how it goes."

It's hard to picture her without a lab coat, let alone tucking a kid into bed.

She flips open her laptop and scrolls around until a picture of a vat of bubbling strawberry jam pops on to the screen. "Here you are."

I don't exactly know what I'm looking at. "Is that my colon?"

"Beautiful, right?" She seems sincere. "The human body. A mystery and a miracle."

"If it's beautiful, why am I sick?"

"Good point. What I mean is that the system is beautiful

in the way we take in nourishment, use what we can, and then get rid of the leftovers." She points to the red blisters in the image. "Your body is not a happy camper. It's fighting against itself, which means, aside from spending a lot of time in the bathroom, you aren't getting the nutrients from the food you do eat." She must see the puzzled look on my face because she pauses. "Did you have a question?"

Yes. I want to ask if my body's fighting against itself because I've stuffed all those emotions about Dad. Would I be sick if I'd talked to Emmett? Is this my own fault? "Can stress cause this?"

She nods. "Stress can *trigger* flare-ups, certainly. But this"—she waves at the computer screen—"is *caused* by something else."

"Like what?"

"Hard to say until we get the labs back. But clearly you've got some sort of bowel inflammation."

It sounds horrible. But anything with *bowel* sounds gross. "What will make it better?"

She makes a click with her tongue. "We need to figure out exactly what it is first. In the meantime, you might want to try a naturopath. They have other tools that might help, like food-allergy testing. I'm guessing certain foods trigger attacks."

"Totchos," I say. "And school pizza."

Dr. Lee closes her laptop. Smiles. "Those were on the

menu back in my day." She sweeps her long hair over her shoulder. I wonder what she was like in middle school. Orchestra kid? Drama nerd? Acting skills probably come in handy for doctors.

"Do you think I'm gluten intolerant?" My cousin used to get bad stomachaches until they figured out she is.

"Celiac disease?" She tilts her head, like Ruffles when she's really listening. "Not likely your issue but, if it turns out you're allergic to gluten, there are a million good recipes these days." She pulls a prescription pad from her pocket, scribbles on it. "Look these up. This is my favorite blogger. Gluten-Free Goddess. Killer brownie cupcakes. Any other questions?"

"When do I get to go home?"

She leans forward, sending a wave of something light and lemony my way. "Job number one is to get you out of here as soon as possible. I promise." She stands. "I'm thinking we can spring you tomorrow. Can you handle one more night?"

Her kindness breaks through my resolve and the tears start. "I'm sorry." I wipe at my eyes.

"Let whatever emotions happen just be." She comes to the side of the bed. "You want to know why I got into this field of medicine?"

"It is kind of . . . a strange choice."

She laughs. "Right. Why not be an OB and deliver

babies? Or an ENT and spend my days peering into ear canals? Instead I get up close and personal with colons."

My laughter releases more tears. I wiggle in the narrow hospital bed, trying to reach the box of tissue.

Dr. Lee hands it over. "I chose this field because, when I was fifteen, I was right where you are. I know it's not fun. Being tied to the bathroom. Packing spare undies. Leaving parties early."

I crumple the tissue, thinking of all Elly's unanswered texts. "Not knowing what to tell your friends."

"I hear you. But there is a path forward. You *will* feel better." She pivots and hands me the water bottle. "Let's work on getting you rehydrated."

"Thanks." I take the bottle. "I mean for telling me."

Her lemon scent lingers long after the door closes.

Chapter 17

"Doesn't this look tasty?" Mom holds out a magazine, nodding toward a cake recipe.

"Whole Orange Cake. Yum." I give her a little jab. "Rip it out."

"Tess." Mom makes a face, but she laughs.

"It's not a federal crime," I say. "Besides, I could bake it for Scott's birthday." A non-Knife twinge hits my stomach when I say "bake." I haven't done anything in over a week except sleep, binge Netflix, and force fluids.

"It's not our magazine. It belongs to the clinic."

"Okay then." I pull out my phone and snap a photo. "Happy?"

"Absolutely."

At least one of us is. I'd rather be working on that final essay for Mrs. Chatterjee than be here.

A kid across the waiting room whines, "It's my turn!" He yanks a game player away from his brother. "Mo—om!"

I put in one earbud, flipping through playlists on my phone. I scroll right past the last one Elly sent me. She's texted a kajillion times since I passed out. Giving me the daily gossip. Reporting Rajit's latest musical crush—"At least it's *Hamilton*"—and delivering the news that the bake sale raised more than enough money for the dance. I haven't answered once. But I will today. For sure. After this appointment. After I find out what's wrong.

Her Elly ESP must be on high alert because my phone pings at that moment.

> Please tell me what's going on!

My thumbs hover over the keyboard.

"Tiffany?"

I swivel my head toward the nurse, even though she's calling a different patient. I check the time. We've been here an eternity. I squirm around on the hard plastic chair, trying to get comfy.

"You're worse than Gracie." Mom pats my leg. "Patience."

Another ping. Elly's taking a poll: Should she listen to Unpaid Pasta or Marmalade Jamb while studying for her French test?

Rajit's typing:

> Neither. West Side Story soundtrack. Only decent music around.

Oh, he's living dangerously.

Now Mom's squirming. "Good thing I asked Scott to pick your sister up today."

"Patience." I pat her leg. "You're worse than Gracie."

"I deserve that." She snags two more magazines from the table. "*Field & Stream* or *Car and Driver*?"

"Definitely *Field & Stream*."

"Tess?" The nurse—her name badge says *Virginia*—stands in the doorway, laptop in hand. "Tess Medina?"

I hop up. Mom does, too. "Um, can you stay here?"

Mom pulls her purse to her side. "Two sets of ears are better than one."

"Fine." I follow the nurse through the open door, pretending Mom's not trailing along behind.

Nurse Virginia points to the exam table. "Have a seat."

The paper crinkles loudly as I sit. Awkward. I squirm to get comfy, but that only makes the paper crease up against the backs of my thighs.

Virginia consults her laptop. "So, you're here for your test results?"

Mom waits for me to answer. But I don't. She wanted to be here; she can run the show. "Yes," she says finally.

After a few more questions, Virginia snaps her laptop shut. "Dr. Lee's running a bit late but should be in shortly."

She leaves and Mom eases onto one of the two blue vinyl chairs, shrugging out of her coat.

I swing my legs, creating my own crumpled table paper

symphony, checking out the room. Beige walls. One framed photo of Mount Rainier. Two posters of the digestive system. A display of assorted brochures: *You and IBD. Vivir Con La Colitis Ulcerosa. Pete Learns all about Crohn's and Colitis.* Blerg. I press my hands to my stomach. What's taking so long?

In four. I visualize pressing oxygen into that knot in my shoulder. Into my legs. My gut. *Out eight.* All this waiting makes me twitchy.

Ping.

I'm worried about U

Yeah, well, Elly, I'm kind of worried about me, too. "Do you think they forgot us?"

Mom sighs and shifts her coat up over her shoulders. "I'm sure she's very busy."

The door swings open a few moments later and, on a gust of lemon, Dr. Lee bursts in. She doesn't waste any time in delivering the news. The bad news. The very bad news.

"Crohn's disease?" I repeat.

Dr. Lee's starched white coat complains as she settles in the chair. "As I mentioned, I was pretty certain you had inflammatory bowel issues. Crohn's is in that family. Affects the lining of the digestive tract, all the way from the mouth to rectum."

Oh my frog. That sounds disgusting. And that's what I tell Dr. Lee.

"Tess!" Mom frowns.

Dr. Lee sets her laptop aside. "It's okay. Tess can be honest with me. And I will be completely honest with her. I think my patients deserve that."

I go all cold and clammy. Mom reaches for my hand, but, accompanied by a crackling paper concerto, I slide out of reach.

Dr. Lee doesn't blink at the family drama. Keeps going. "Crohn's is a chronic disease."

Mom tightens her grip on her purse.

"You mean, doesn't go away? Ever?" Now I wish I had taken her hand. I could use something to hang on to.

Dr. Lee adjusts the stethoscope draped around her neck. "And there's no cure. Yet."

The room tilts forty-five degrees. I'm going to puke. No cure. I'm stuck with the Knife for the rest of my life. Even though my brain knows it's not her fault, I refuse to look at Dr. Lee. I want out of here.

"But it is possible to control the flares. I think you're a good candidate for Remicade. I'd like to start you on that." Dr. Lee explains that the drug attacks a protein that seems to cause the kind of inflammation I've got.

"An injection?" Mom asks.

"Infusion. All administered by IV; the treatment rooms are here at the hospital. After the initial three monthly doses, they'll only be every two months." As if this is something to be happy about.

I can sense Mom's glance. Even if I wanted to talk, I can't form words. There is no spit in my mouth. I close my eyes and pretend it's happening to someone else. Someone who's not signed up for a baking competition in two months.

"How long does the treatment last?" Mom asks the question I can't.

"A couple of hours, each time."

"I meant, how long—" I hear Mom's hands brushing her jeans.

"Oh, I see." The lab coat sighs. "Forever. Or until it stops working. But if it does, we try something else."

Mom makes an odd choking sound.

"I will do my utmost to ensure Tess lives a full, normal life." Dr. Lee's given up on talking to me. I know what she's saying: *Look at me. I'm normal.* But instead of helping, the words tick me off. And someone needs to tell her that lemon perfume smells like air freshener.

Mom fumbles with her coat. "This is a lot to process. May we call with questions later?"

"Of course." Dr. Lee stands. Ruin Tess's life: check. Her work here is done.

My back pocket buzzes. I yank out my phone. Power it off.

"Thank you, Dr. Lee." Mom shakes her hand.

I burst out of the exam room and make a beeline for the car, but of course it's locked. I'm sure everyone in the parking lot's staring as I wait for Mom.

While I'm getting buckled, Mom studies me: *Over here, in this cage, kid with an embarrassing disease.* "You okay?"

"Yes, Mother, just fine. Thanks for asking." I jam the buckle into the latch. "Best news I've had all year."

She slumps behind the wheel. "I'm so, so sorry."

I press my forehead to the cool glass of the window. I'm being a brat, I know. But it's all I've got right now. "It's not fair."

"No, it's not."

"I can't even tell anybody about it. It's so gross." I shudder. "Will you homeschool me? Please?"

"Oh, honey." Mom pushes my hair back over my shoulder. "This won't keep you from doing what you want. *Whatever* you want. Didn't you hear Dr. Lee say that?"

"She isn't in middle school." My life is over. Oh. Ver. "And what about the bake-off? How's that going to happen?"

The silence sucks all the air out of the car. Mom eventually speaks. "I don't know, but we'll get through this."

We? I'm the one with the Knife carving me up. The one who'll never be able to go to a movie. Or a sleepover. And forget the stupid dance. Or the bake-off. I can see it now:

Oh, excuse me, judges, while I poop my guts out. "Can we just go home? Now?"

After a long pause, she starts the car. "I know it's hard, but you've got Dr. Lee—and us—on your side."

A pep talk is the last thing I need. "Home. Please." I swipe at my eyes.

Mom pushes the ignition button. "How about we binge watch the *British Baking Show*? Invite Elly over?" This is her bribe-Gracie-with-a-cookie voice. When I think it can't get any worse, I'm reduced to being treated like a four-year-old.

I pivot toward the window, and even though I squeeze my eyes tight, tears squeak through. The only sound on the car ride home is the occasional sniffle from either side of the front seat.

Gracie and Scott wait on the front porch. Gracie barrels up to the car, pigtails bouncing. "Tessie! Is your tummy all better?"

"Whoa there, tiger!" Mom slides out of the driver's seat. "Let's give your sister a little space. She'll talk to you later." She steers her back inside.

I slump forward, head on the dash, unable to stop watching the mental movie of my new life. Reel after reel of infusions and doctor visits and never being more than fifty feet from a bathroom. Oh yes, and more colonoscopies to look forward to. Every year. Double yay.

I grab my phone and text.

> No matter what Dr. Lee says, there's no normal in my future. What's the point in even getting out of the car?

I stare at the screen then shove my phone into my pocket.

It's true. About the car. The seats lean back. Mom keeps bottled water in the trunk and enough Gracie snacks stashed in the glove box to keep me going a week. Maybe longer. Like, forever. I spread out on the seat. Get comfy. As comfy as I can.

Tap tap tap.

"Mom. Leave me alone."

"It's me." Elly presses her nose against the glass.

"What are you doing here?" My tone's so ugly, I'm surprised Elly doesn't storm off.

She flashes her phone. "Fifty-seven unanswered texts. Your mom said I could come over."

"Go away." I pull my hoodie over my head. "I want to wallow."

"Proper wallowing should never be done solo." Elly is a rhinoceros. There is no moving her if she doesn't want to be moved. "Look. I'm here for you."

I edge away from the window. Tug on my hoodie strings.

Elly says nothing for a long time. A remarkable length of time, considering it's Elly.

She taps again. Gently. With her fingertips. Like she's patting a small, scared creature. "Can't you tell me what's going on?"

I wobble my head.

"Can I come in?"

I can barely breathe in here. Not adding another body.

"You are freaking me out."

She does sound scared. Sure, I'm some kind of chronic case, but I don't have to be a complete jerk. "Okay, fine. But don't even think about trying to make me feel better."

Elly climbs in the back. "Wouldn't dream of it. Here's my plan. We go to your room, kill the lights, and rock out to The Smiths."

"It's no joke, El." We catch each other's eyes in the rearview mirror. Another tear dribbles off my chin. "I don't want to talk about it. Ever."

Elly reaches over the seat to rest her hand on my shoulder. The warmth transfers through my hoodie and into my heart. "I respect that. But I am here for you. Also. Maybe you *should* tell me. In case something happens when we're together. Do I need to brush up on my CPR?"

"El." We are not going to be together. I'm not going anywhere she would want to go.

She pats the head rest. "Sorry. I can't help it. I blather when I don't know what to say."

"It's okay to say nothing."

"Right. Got that. Making a note." She flops backward. "Maybe I should get a tattoo? Then I'd never forget."

"I can see you all tatted up."

"Obviously not for a few more years. I think you have to be eighteen. Or sixteen with a parent's permission, but that's never going to happen." She claps her hand over her mouth. "No more talking. I promise."

"You can talk. It's okay." I crack the window.

But she doesn't talk. Silent Elly is way harder to deal with than chatty Elly. Finally, she speaks. "So I don't have to be Sherlock Holmes to figure out something's wrong. I mean. Fainting at school." She sits up tall so I can see her in the rearview. "And, got it. We are not discussing whatever 'it' is."

"Absolutely not."

She clears her throat. "The thing is, everyone has something wonky, right? Rajit's crooked teeth, Brooklyn's diabetes, my inability to stop talking when I should. Even your perfect Emmett has some flaws. I mean. Seriously. Tenley?"

"He is NOT my Emmett."

"The point is." She exhales vigorously. "The point is you can't be human without being messed up in some way. Whatever is messed up in you, we'll deal with it. Emphasis on the *we*."

That's easy for her to say because she doesn't know what Crohn's is. I can just see it now: "Oh, Elly, I've pooped myself. Can you grab the spare undies out of my backpack?" N.O.T. Happening. "It's too depressing." I hunker down on the seat.

"Well." Elly leans forward again. "My mom says when you're blue, it helps to do something for others."

"There's nothing you can do to cheer me up."

"Don't be selfish." Elly bats me on the head. "I'm talking about me. My best friend is ghosting me and it's bringing me low."

"I'm the sick one."

She ignores me. "And what would cheer *me* up is your double-chocolate chip cookies."

The car is really stuffy. I peel off my hoodie. "Not in the mood."

She unlatches the passenger door. "Then I will make them myself. With your new cookie sheets."

"You wouldn't."

"Try me." She hops out and sprints to the front door.

Even though there's a forty-pound sack of sad sitting on my shoulders, I haul my flawed, sick body out of the car to save my new bakeware.

Besides, a cookie does sound kind of good.

Chapter 18

I can't come up with one solid argument to convince Mom to let me stay home another day. "You don't want to have to repeat eighth grade, do you?" She hands me a glass of water.

"No. Once is enough. But did you see that link I sent you? To that online school?"

She drops a couple pills in my hand. "Take these and get going."

Maybe I can sneak into school without any fuss. Maybe I'll fade into the motivating walls—YOUR ATTITUDE WILL DETERMINE YOUR DIRECTION!—invisible to the eye.

My hope for a covert re-entry gets shut down the moment I step through the main doors.

Two puffy pink arms flail in my direction. "Tess!" Elly suffocates me against her Michelin Man down jacket. "I have missed you sooo much!"

"You were over at my house on Friday," I point out.

"Eons ago." She tugs on my backpack. "What did you bake for us today?"

"Oh, that's all you care about?"

She fake-stabs herself in the heart. Stumbles back.

"Varlet! Thou hast slain me with thy words." After a second, she grabs my arm. "Well, yes, I missed your cookies. They're addictive. And delicious. But I missed your sparkling wit ever so much more."

"So you're not interested in any Peanut Butter Dreams?"

"I didn't say that!"

"Not in so many words." I raise an eyebrow. Laugh. It feels amazing to joke around. To be normal. But the laughing gets me coughing.

Her face turns serious. Intense. "How are you feeling?"

I'd broken down and told her everything when she came over, and now she's turned Mama Bear. But I wouldn't mind a slice of that protection when it comes to getting through the next six hours. You don't get taken away by ambulance, sirens blaring and lights spinning, without everyone in the school noticing. Even the kids who'd been absent that day have heard about it, the middle school grapevine being the fastest existing form of communication. Another reason for my recent vacation from social media: not up for seeing my life dissected like a paramecium.

I know Elly cares. "Super-duper. Really." I point to a nearby poster. IF I CAN DREAM IT, I CAN DO IT.

"Right." Eye roll. "Are you nervous?"

"About?" I pretend not to understand. But she knows there's something I'm really dreading. Or, rather, someone.

"Whatever." She waits a beat then pulls out her phone and hands me her earbuds. "You have *got* to listen to this."

It's less awkward than I'd imagined. I pass a couple of my teachers in the hall and they say they're happy to see me. Ms. Daley gives me a card with a picture of a French bakery on the front. Inside, it says, *If you need to talk, I'm here.*

I'll never, ever take her up on that offer, but I thank her anyway. She gives me a sad smile as if she can read my mind. Ms. Daley really likes helping people.

I pause outside homeroom. *Inhale four. Exhale eight.*

"Hey, Tess." Wayne reaches in front of me to open the door. "I hope you're feeling better."

"Thanks." I bend to pet Rexi then walk through, hoping to make it to my seat without being noticed. But I can't help looking over at Tenley.

Mom brought me blank cards in the hospital so I could write thank-yous to all the people who'd helped, like Alix and the other nurses. Dr. Lee. The social worker Lourdes. And Tenley. She saved me from breaking my nose, dialed 911 from her cell, and stayed till the medics came. Writing the note hadn't felt weird. But the thought of facing her in person is a twenty on a scale of one to ten. Fifty.

"Ms. Bread Science!" Emmett pulls out my desk chair for me. "Doing okay?"

Someday I may talk to Emmett about Dad, but no way am I touching the subject of Crohn's. "Yeah. Good. Thanks. That was a nice card you and Ruffles sent. I didn't know you were such an artist." He'd drawn a picture of Mabel on the inside.

"Me and Picasso." He grins. "It's not that good. But I appreciate the compliment. Glad you're back." He pats my desk and turns to join Wayne in trash talking about some basketball game.

I smile to acknowledge Bethany's "Welcome back," still avoiding anything or anyone in Tenley's general direction. But it's like when you're little and lose a tooth and can't keep your tongue away from the hole. I catch her eye and she looks away, kind of like she's dreading this encounter, too. Better get it over with.

"Those look good." Her streaks are now orange.

"Going for a tigress vibe." She tucks a piece behind her ear.

I stand there; she studies her thumb. Flakes off chipped purple polish. "That was a nice note."

"My mom said you saved me from a concussion. Or worse."

She shrugs. "Like I said. Tigress."

"Well—" I'm not sure what else to say.

"So. I hope you're feeling better."

"Thanks."

"Cool." Clearly, end of discussion. But it's okay. It's not like we're going to totally bond over this. Become besties. That only happens in sappy novels.

At lunch, Elly slides her tray on to the table but avoids eye contact.

"Everything okay?" I ask.

"Perfect." Her leg jiggles while she doctors up a baked potato.

"Elly." Rajit's voice contains a warning. What's going on?

"I know." She blobs on some sour cream then drops her fork. "Okay. I can't stand it any longer."

"What?" I salt my hard-boiled egg.

Elly drumrolls on the table. "Guess who's coming to Portland?"

Rajit throws up his hands. "You suck at secrets."

"Front-row seats!" Elly gives me a shake. "For the competition!"

"Your own cheering section." Rajit waves imaginary pom-poms.

"Seriously?"

They both nod. Elly crosses her heart. "Dad's going to drive us down right after school on the Friday before. Wayne's coming, too!"

I turn away, blinking. I can't cry. Not at school. "You guys are the best. You really are."

Elly claps her hands. "We might even get T-shirts made!"

"Oh. No. Don't do that!" I spin back around.

She's laughing. "Buttons? Balloons? Temporary tattoos?"

"Stop her," I beg Rajit.

"Do not worry." He flexes his biceps. "I'll keep her on a leash."

"You wish!" Elly flips her ponytail.

"No, *I* wish." I press my hands into prayer pose.

Elly pouts. "Baseball caps? Face paint? Kazoos?"

"Don't even." I cover my eyes.

"All right. All right. I will be über chill. I promise." She holds out her pinky.

"Swear?" I twine my pinky with hers.

"Swear."

But I don't trust her Cheshire Cat smile.

Chapter 19

The elevator doors swish open and I look for the blue line. Blue leads to the infusion room. That's what the instructions said. The coral line leads to the coffee shop, which is where I'd rather go. Mom and I play follow the leader with blue as it winds down halls, turns corners, past staffed desks and busy people. We step aside for a pacing girl hooked up to an IV pole. Nearby, a couple of women chat happily over fancy coffees.

The line eventually leads us to a window decorated with tiny blinking green and white lights for St. Patrick's Day and a woman wearing a four-leaf clover headband over her dreadlocks. "Checking in?"

"Tess Medina."

She clicks around on the keyboard. "Looks like you're here for an infusion. Sound right?"

My voice sticks in my throat so I nod.

More keyboard clicking. The printer spits out page after page and then a long line of fluorescent green stickers. She sticks one on a wristband. "Can I have your right arm, please?"

The wristband's a flashing light announcing, *Disease Disease Disease.* I tuck it up under my sweatshirt sleeve, silencing the alarm.

"Now, Mom, is it? Here are the insurance forms and hospital waivers. Please fill them out and sign at the bottom. You can work on that in the waiting room if you like. The infusion takes a couple of hours, so feel free to go grab a coffee. This month's special is an Irish Cream latte. Use this to get a dollar off." She hands Mom a coupon. "When you're ready, the blue line brings you back to us."

Mom tucks her purse under her arm. "You want me to stay?"

I shrug my hands farther into my sleeves. "I'll be fine. I have homework." And Elly's special playlist. She made me pinky swear not to listen until I got here.

"Well, call if you need anything." Mom doesn't move, though, like she's playing frozen tag with Gracie.

"We'll take excellent care of her," the receptionist says. "I promise."

That unfreezes her. She gives me a quick kiss on the cheek. "I'll grab a chamomile tea for you for after. Do you want a cookie, too?"

"Tess Medina?" A nurse walks up.

"That's me." I turn to Mom. "Just tea, please." I don't know if it's the thermostat or the ambience; no matter what they do to hospitals, they always feel like blast chillers.

"I'm Jeremy. This way." I follow, eyes down. If I can avoid looking around this place, maybe it won't be real. But it is real. And I'm shivering as if I'd done the polar bear plunge. We pass through one room where fake leather recliner chairs form a crooked U; Jeremy slows by an empty seat. Mine?

But we keep walking, past the recliners and down another hall. Jeremy takes a hard right into a small room. Four chairs, all empty. My shoulders loosen a little. I won't have to chat with anyone. Smell anyone's Starbucks. All by myself, I could almost imagine this is not happening.

Jeremy waves me to a chair. "This will be yours for the next few hours, so get comfy."

I sit down, rubbing my hands up and down my arms, wishing I'd brought another sweatshirt.

"It can get pretty chilly in here, so holler and I'll bring you a blanket." He sidles up to the computer by the chair.

Is it too early to holler? I'm freezing.

"Can you please verify the information on your bracelet?"

I pull out my arm and take a quick glance. "It looks good." Well, if good means a neon sign screaming "sick kid."

"Great." His cheerfulness as he reads off my name and birth date belongs in an ice cream parlor, not a hospital. "And you're here for a Remicade infusion?"

I force my teeth to stop chattering to answer. "Yes."

"Ordered by Dr. Lee, for the diagnosis of Crohn's?"

"Yes." I've been asked these questions a million times these last few weeks. Why can't they keep track of the answers? What are they using those computers for anyway?

"Chatty thing, aren't ya?" Jeremy stops clicking.

My lips slide up in a courtesy grin.

"Okay." He rolls his chair from the computer toward me. "Let's see what we have to work with, shall we?"

I pull my sleeve up over a fading bruise. Proof of the trauma my arm endured when I was in the hospital. But evidently that's not enough. More poking to come.

Jeremy tightens a band around my bicep. My upper arm begins to ache, but I know by now to squeeze my fist tight. "This'll work." He wipes down my inner elbow with a cold swab.

The alcohol smell makes me want to puke. I wish I hadn't had that mango smoothie on the way. But Mom insisted I put some food in my stomach. Last time I'm listening to her.

"Let me give you the rundown on how this will work. First, I'll put in the line."

"Like an IV?" I know what that's like.

"Almost." Jeremy gestures in the air. "With the IV, we insert a hollow-nose needle that allows the solution to go through. With this, I need to slide a tiny tube into the vein."

Mango bubbles up my throat.

"Once that's good to go, I order your medicine." He swivels the chair side to side. "It's frustrating, but you'll probably have to wait a while for it to come up. The minute it gets here, though, I'll begin your drip. Full force for about an hour, then I'll add a little saline at the end to make sure we get every last drop." Does he have to be so peppy? He swivels again. "Any questions?"

Yes, I want to say. Can I leave now? But I shake my head. No questions, Your Honor. The sooner I get used to this, the better. Part of my new "normal."

"Okay. Deep breath, then exhale. On the count of three."

I wince as the tube goes in. Pressure builds as he threads the line; it feels like he's trying to shove a straw into my vein. I tug the cuff of the sweatshirt sleeve on my other hand and crumple it tighter and tighter in my palm until he's done. Pure relief as the armband is loosened and he finishes up. "There, that was easy, huh?"

I don't give him the courtesy smile this time. It wasn't easy. And my arms are going to look like Mabel, full of woodpecker holes.

"Okay, I'll go submit that order. I'll be back as soon as I can to hook you up to the meds."

"I'll be here." As if I'm going anywhere hooked up like this.

He chuckles. "Need anything? Magazine?"

I hold up my notebook. "Got it covered. Homework. Thanks."

"Oh, the blanket. One or two?"

I don't want to sound greedy. "One is fine."

A few seconds later, he's back. "Seems like a two-blanket day." He hands me one to put over my lap and drapes the other one around my shoulders. At least I'm warm. Muffled voices page doctors, call codes. I don't even want to know what code silver is. Squeaky carts roll by. Someone down the hall laughs in three sharp barks, like a seal.

I need a distraction so I flip open my notebook. Mom thought this would be the perfect time to do some prewriting for the LA final essay. She has a funny idea of "perfect time." The topic is "A Defining Moment in My Life." Definitely not from Walmart but oh my frog. A defining moment? I look around me. This sure counts. But getting an infusion is the last thing I want to write about. Learning to bake? That involves Dad. Kryptonite. I stare at the blank page until all the lines melt away and everything is empty. Like my brain.

Time to go to my happy place. I pull out my earbuds and phone and hit play.

The first thing I hear is Wayne's voice. "Rexi and I picked our favorite song. It's the one—"

"Shh." Rajit talks over him. "It's supposed to be a surprise." He coughs. Twice. "Tess. I have done my best to save you from the wackadoodle music choices of our other mutual friend. She allowed me to contribute a total of two, that's right, two tracks to this playlist. The tasteful ones, the—"

Elly interrupts. "Without further ado, we present the Doody List, made with love for our favorite Crohn's patient."

The first track launches: "Ode de Toilet," by Brad Paisley. Wayne and Rexi's pick. Then come Rajit's contributions—"Easy Street" from *Annie* and "Defying Gravity" from *Wicked*. But every other song is about toilets.

Every. Single. One.

I love my friends.

Chapter 20

"Assistant dog walker reporting for duty! Hi, Mrs. Medina." Elly homes in on the still-warm biscuits. "Oh, those look scrummy!"

I pass her a plate and the butter dish. "Jam?"

Butter melts onto her hand. "Perfect as is." She inhales a second biscuit.

"Are you sure you're up to this?" Mom taps her fingers against her coffee cup. If I had a dollar for every time she's asked this lately, I could buy another Bernice. "It's only been a week since your infusion."

"Twelve days," I remind her. "And I got ten hours of sleep last night."

"Rest you really need if you're going to the bake-off in, what"—she glances at the calendar—"three weeks."

"Not *if*," I say. "When."

Elly washes off her buttery hands. "I've watched three YouTubes on first aid."

"See? Elly's got my back." And she does. The first time we went to the new mall after my diagnosis, she'd downloaded a map and highlighted all the bathrooms.

Mom's mug clinks against the counter. "I have no doubt about that. I worry—"

"Which you don't need to do." I hug her. "Seriously. I will admit, the first couple days after the infusion were rough, but I'm fine now." I stare straight at her. "Fine."

"Ready?" Elly asks.

I stuff the baggie full of dog treats into my pocket. "All set."

"Finish your protein shake," Mom says. "You have your phone?"

"Glued to my hand." I drain the shake.

"Very funny. Don't be gone too long. You need to work on that essay."

As if I need reminding. Ugh. Mom waves us off and, a few minutes later, we're headed toward the park. Elly's handling Trixie and I've got Peanut. Both dogs stop to sniff the base of a stop sign. It's a warmish day for late March, overcast but no rain. For a change.

"Reading their pee mail." Elly grins. "Did you know dogs' sense of smell is, like, ten thousand times better than ours? And that they have eighteen muscles controlling their ears? And they can hear sounds farther away than humans can?"

"Someone did a little googling," I tease.

"Well, I've never had a dog. I figured I should learn about them if I'm going to be your assistant." Elly tugs Trixie away from a cigarette butt.

"You look like a natural."

Elly stumbles as Trixie yanks her toward a rhododendron.

"Some dogs can pull eight times their weight." I share one of the dog facts I know.

"I believe it." Elly rubs her shoulder. "Heel, Trixie." Trixie tugs in the other direction.

"I don't think she knows 'heel.'" I make kissy noises and bribe Trixie with a treat.

"Let me try." Elly takes a handful and repeats what I did. "Hey, look. It works!"

Trixie mostly trots beside Elly the rest of the way to the park. The sun breaks through the clouds, shining on the path. I point. "That looks like an invitation."

"We can say hi to Mabel and then maybe turn around? Doable?"

"Doable." And it is, but I don't want to push it. If I come home wiped out, Mom will freak out. "I do kind of need to save my energy for the bake-off."

"What's left to practice?" Elly asks. "You've checked everything off the list."

"My last batch of pastry cream was a lumpy disaster," I remind her. "And let's not forget the burned caramel."

"Piffle!" She waves those off.

"Piffle?" I repeat.

"Sounds English, don't you think?" She fakes a British

accent. "Everything you bake is perfectly scrummy and you know it. And soon, everyone will know it because—" She shakes my arm. "You are going to win the bake-off!"

"I do make a mean macaron."

"And everything else." We crunch along, the dogs crisscrossing the path in front of us. I don't know what she's thinking about, but I'm thinking about Dad. And winning for him. I could do it. I really could.

Elly reaches her maximum allowable period of silence. "I thought there were fairies in this forest when I was little. I even told my class I saw one." She laughs self-consciously. "Got razzed about it all through second grade."

"I totally believe you saw one. This place is magical."

She nudges me with her shoulder. "Spoken like a true friend."

"I keep thinking it'd be fun to build a fairy house for Gracie to find."

"Oh, I want in on that! Right there. That's the perfect place." Elly tugs Trixie closer to a rotted stump. "It already has a moss carpet!"

"You are a goof." I'm really touched by how much Elly cares about Gracie. I let out Peanut's leash so he can sniff around Mabel. But I don't let him pee on her. Seems disrespectful. I think it would also hurt Emmett's feelings.

Elly wrestles a candy wrapper away from Trixie. "You know how I like to look stuff up?"

"Like learning everything canine for a one-time dog walking job?"

She snorts. "Yeah. Okay. A bit of overkill. But you've gotta admit dogs are fascinating. I mean, they've been humans' best friends for nearly thirty thousand years." She works out a twig caught in Trixie's fur. "Anyway, I sent away for information. From the Crohn's & Colitis Foundation."

"O-kayyy."

"Also signed up for their newsletter. There's tons of research going on, Tess."

I rub my hand against Mabel's trunk, tracing the grooves and divots. "I know. Dr. Lee's big in the field. She's conducting some trials for a drug that could work for me, down the road." I let my hand linger to soak up Mabel's solidness. Her "thereness."

"Maybe she'll find a cure. If anyone could, it'd be her," Elly says confidently.

"Maybe." I pull a weed near Mabel's plaque. "We should get going."

"So anyway, there's this walk. You know. To raise money. I thought you, me, Raj, and Wayne could be a team."

When I was Gracie's age, I loved building stick dams across the tiny creek near our house, watching the water back up before knocking down the sticks so the creek could swoosh over my creation. That's the rush I feel right now. I clear my throat. "You don't have to."

"Have to? It's *want* to." Now she slugs me. "What? We're not friends?"

"Don't be a dork." I can't believe Elly would put herself in the situation of asking people to donate for such an embarrassing disease. I blink. Everything makes me cry lately.

"Anyway, I've already picked our team name."

"I can't wait."

"Picture this in white on purple." Elly cocks her head in a perfect imitation of Trixie. She pauses. "Purple is the color of this particular cause. Not my favorite but we'll work with it."

"I'm sure they'll consult you next time." The air is lighter. Partly because we're headed out of the trees and partly because of her.

She and Trixie hop over a log blocking the path. Peanut and I walk around; too much for his short legs.

"Are you ready?" Elly waits till we catch up.

"I'm a bit terrified—"

"Don't worry. It's clean. Wa-ait for it." She makes blinking motions with her hand, like a marquee light. "'Gut Reaction.'"

I laugh.

"So you like it?" Her face begs for a yes.

"Considering all the other names you could've chosen, this one's awesome." I give a thumbs-up. "I hate asking people for money, though. Even for good causes. I couldn't sell Thin Mints to save my life when I was a Brownie." Dad ended up buying two cases and gave them away at the bakery to help me out.

"People like to do good. You just have to think of the right way to ask." She leads the way across the street, away from the park. "We can say we want to 'relieve' them of their money for a good cause. Or that regular elimination of cash is good for the system. Or they can 'dump' their spare change. Or—"

I hold up my free hand. "Yeah. No." I laugh. "You are so full of it."

And she is.

In the best way.

Chapter 21

A week before the bake-off, I'm shivering under my blankets. It feels like my blood's been replaced with Slushees. Maybe I shouldn't have tried tackling both a vertical lemon blueberry cake and Napoleons today.

"Want to play Pioneer?" Gracie tugs on my covers.

"I'm resting." I pull them back up.

"How about Barbie?" She somersaults across the bed, barely missing my face with her feet. I move them away.

"Maybe tomorrow? I'm kind of wiped right now."

She somersaults onto the floor. "You were too tired yesterday, too."

I close my eyes. Yesterday it was espresso cheesecake and lemon doughnuts topped with marble glaze. And after school Friday, I made a red velvet cake, orange sweet rolls, and a salted caramel tart. All good reasons to be tired. "It's the last week before the bake-off and I'm working hard to get ready, that's all."

"It's bad to get tired, right, Tessie?" Gracie leans over me, exhaling graham cracker breath as she pats my cheek.

"Daddy died because his heart got tired. That's what Mommy says."

Her words are a gut punch. "Yeah, well, he had a heart attack." Oh my frog. I don't think I can handle this conversation right now.

She picks Owlie up and hugs him close. "You're tired, but your heart is okay. It's your tummy that hurts."

Her expression shreds me to the core, and I finally get it. I sit up, scoop her onto my lap. "I'm not going to die, Gracie." I tap her nose. "My body gets tired. But my heart is super-duper."

"I thought so." She plops Owlie next to my head. "Owlie and I will make you all better."

"Thanks, peanut."

She wanders out and, a few minutes later, skips back carrying her Fisher-Price teapot and a broken teacup. The teapot croaks out a song as Gracie pours. "Here you go." She offers it to me.

I take a pretend sip. "Yum. I'll drink the rest later. Can you put it on my desk?"

She does. "Don't let it get cold."

"I won't." Let me close my eyes for a minute. One sweet minute.

"Am I a good nurse?" she asks.

"A very good nurse. Now I need to rest." I snuggle deeper in the bed.

* * *

I startle when the door swings open.

"Tess? Dinner's ready." Mom turns on my desk lamp.

I blink. "I guess I fell asleep."

"Maybe you overdid it this weekend?"

"It's getting down to the wire. I gotta bring my A game to Portland."

Mom smooths the covers. "Hungry?"

"Later? Maybe cinnamon toast?"

She gets up. Straightens the Florence and the Machine poster Elly gave me, neatens the stack of books on my desk. Fiddles with the blinds. Then, she leans against my dresser. "Tess. I know this bake-off is important to you. But your health is far more important."

I tighten Owlie's scarf. "It takes a while for the infusions to work. Remember?"

"If the bake-off was after you've had a couple more infusions, more time for things to calm down—"

"And, okay, maybe I overdid it this weekend," I say.

"Honey, can you see yourself competing, feeling like this?" She waves her hand over me.

Could I? Not right this minute. But Dr. Lee promised normal. "I've been drinking those protein shakes. Staying hydrated. Everything Dr. Lee told me to do."

"I know. I know. You've been the perfect patient, but—"

I slap my hands on the bedspread. "She said I would

have a normal life. Normal! And that means doing the things that are part of *my* normal." I'm shivering again, now from being mad as well as cold.

"It's just the timing. Next year might be better."

My pulse swooshes in my ears, as loud as Bernice's motor. "Next year won't be the tenth anniversary. I might not be invited."

"Oh, you'd win a spot. Those macarons of yours are to die for." This is Mom's cheerleader voice. She uses it to say things like: *Well, any party you're not invited to can't be much of a party. Well, even Einstein failed a math test or two. Well, I bet Mary Berry's burnt her share of jelly rolls.* She pats my leg. "Don't you think waiting would be the best decision?"

I swear I catch a whiff of Doublemint. Maybe only in my imagination, but who cares? I sit up. "Learning to live with the Knife starts by going to the bake-off."

She studies her flip-flops for a long time. Then she lifts her head, her smile blinking on and off like a dying lightbulb. "I've been planning all day for a way to tell you that I'm not letting you go."

Another stab in my gut. Not the Knife. Disappointment. "Mom—"

"Wait. Let me finish." She fishes something out of her pocket. Sets it next to me.

Dad's phone.

"I just need to hear his voice sometimes, you know? He'd drive me crazy with those dorky puns."

"Totally dorky." My heart's pinched in my chest. "And totally Dad."

She pulls back her hair. "I know. Right? What a goof. And I'm a goof, too, because I keep paying the phone bill."

Oh my frog. Why didn't I think about this before? She saw the texts! "Mom, let me explain."

She plunks down on the edge of the bed. Presses her hand on mine.

"It was stupid." I grab a corner of the sheet to wipe my tears.

"No more stupid than dialing his number to hear that terrible pun." She grabs the other edge of the sheet and blots her own face. "Besides, it took seeing those messages for me to get it. You're his daughter, through and through. I always want to honor and support that." She sniffles. "Which means, I need to let you go to the competition, not keep you from it. Sorry I've been so slow to figure that out."

"Sorry I make you worry." Our heads tilt together and we sit quietly for a time. "I'll be okay, really."

"He got such a kick out of you copying everything he did." She chuckles. "That's what got him to quit smoking, you know. He was afraid you'd try it."

"He was a really great dad," I say.

"A really, really great one."

"And you know I adore Scott."

"Completely understood."

"Thanks, Mom."

She grabs my hand. "So, what do you say? Are you going to bake your heart out next weekend?"

I squeeze. One, two, three. "Do you even have to ask that question?"

She snort-laughs. Grabs a tissue. Blows her nose. "Here's an idea. You stay put. I'll bring that cinnamon toast."

"And some real tea?" I nod at the fake teacup.

Mom pauses in the doorway. "Two spoons of sugar?"

"Perfect." I grab Owlie and nestle back down in my bed.

Chapter 22

My head bobs as I doze in the car. I had a rocky night and, when I did sleep, my dreams were full of baking fails. Like forgetting the sugar or burning the caramel sauce or cutting my hand too badly to continue.

"Are we there yet?" Gracie slips off her headphones and kicks the back of Scott's seat.

"Remember? First, we cross the high, high bridge. Then we'll be in Oregon." Mom signals to change lanes.

"You doing okay?" Scott massages the back of her neck.

"The big question is, how is our champion doing?" She glances in the rearview mirror.

"Ready to get out of the car." That's as much as I want to admit. I don't know whether to blame my queasiness on motion sickness or the Knife.

"Me too." Gracie flaps a coloring book at me. "Should I color the mermaid or the astronaut?"

"The astronaut is cool." I hand her one of the markers she's dropped on the seat between us.

"Her helmet's going to be blue," she says. "My favorite color." She scrubs the marker across the page.

A bridge span looms a few miles ahead. I don't say anything so Gracie can see it first.

A few seconds pass.

"You might want to look out the window," Mom singsongs.

Gracie's head jerks up. She bounces in her car seat. "Look, Tessie. The bridge."

"Sharp eyes." It doesn't take much to make Gracie happy. Ice cream. Noodley Men. Being the first one to spy a bridge. "That's the Columbia River below us."

"It's so big," Gracie exclaims.

"Quick! Hands up!" I lift mine toward the roof. "Make a wish!"

Gracie scrunches her eyes shut. "I'm wishing."

I catch Mom's eye in the rearview. Making a wish on bridges or in tunnels was a total Dad thing. Just because Gracie doesn't remember doesn't mean I can't teach her.

"No telling, otherwise the wish won't come true," I say.

Gracie opens her eyes and blinks, a solemn little owl. "Okay."

After a few wrong turns and many curse words, we find the hotel.

"I am so not a fan of one-way streets." Mom pops the back hatch.

"This is your party, Tess," Scott says. "You should check us in."

The lady at the front desk calls me Miss Medina and hands over a swag bag. "Oh, and here's one for your sous-chef." She holds up a smaller bag for Gracie.

"Presents!"

"Manners?" Scott asks.

"Thank you." Gracie holds the bag close.

Mom tugs her ponytails. "Wasn't that thoughtful?"

The receptionist slides across several key cards and explains what time breakfast is and where. "And here's the information on schedules and so forth from the Jubilee Flour folks. There's a small reception for contestants only beginning at five, then a welcome pizza party for friends and family at six. That all takes place in Ballroom A, on the second floor. Can I help you with anything else?"

I glance over at Mom and Scott but they shake their heads. "I guess we're good," I say.

"Have a wonderful stay. And break a leg at the bake-off." The receptionist laughs. "Or what would one say to wish a baker good luck? May the yeast be with you?"

I smile politely and we cram into the elevator with our bags. "Do you think it's okay if Elly and the guys come to the pizza party?" I ask.

Mom shrugs. "No idea. Is there an information number on that paper the receptionist gave you?"

"I'll check it out after I dump my stuff in the room."

Gracie goes bananas over the picture of the pool in the elevator. "Swim! Swim!" she squeals.

"I think there's time. Want to join us?" The elevator doors slide open and Mom steps out.

"This way," Scott says.

"I think I'll chill." I roll my new suitcase from Mrs. Medcalf along the corridor.

When we get to our room, Mom fumbles open the door. Gracie pushes past to jump on the beds. "Which one do I get?" she asks.

"You pick." Scott unfolds a luggage rack from the closet.

After trying both, Gracie goes for the one nearest the window.

"And you're through here." Mom unlocks the door to the adjoining room. "Is this okay?"

I've never had a hotel room to myself. "Very okay." I roll my suitcase through and look around. A comfy chair covered in an elephant print calls out and I plop down.

Mom finds the mini-fridge behind a wooden door and slides the small cooler bag off her shoulder. "Here you go."

I put away the dairy-free protein shakes. "Home sweet home."

Mom starts through to the other room, then pauses. "How are you feeling?"

"Fine. Well, kind of nervous." I'm pretty sure that's what's going on with my stomach.

"I've never heard you turn down a chance to swim before."

"Saving my energy for the bake-off." Which is ninety-nine percent true.

She pats the doorframe. "We'll probably be back before you leave, but if not, we'll see you in Ballroom A at six." The heavy privacy door does nothing to muffle Gracie singing, "Just keep swimming! Just keep swimming!"

I feel very grown-up. So instead of tearing into the swag bag, I put my clothes in the drawers and set out my stuff in the bathroom. Then I read the schedule: Tomorrow, everything starts at ten, a huge gift. Mornings are especially tough because the Knife isn't a fan of up and at 'em. The morning round lasts till noon, with a break for lunch, and then one round in the afternoon. Everything's done by five. Sunday starts at eight thirty, but I'll deal. The semifinal goes till eleven thirty; lunch break, then the championship round. The closing ceremonies are at four. After that, we hit the road for the three-hour drive home. Sunday's going to be a killer. Maybe Mom will let me skip school on Monday. Or at least first period.

Finally, I let myself peek in the swag bag: an offset spatula with my name engraved on the handle, nesting teaspoons, some yeast packets, and two Theo chocolate bars. I break off one square and nibble. Oh my frog: so good.

I check out the bed. The sheets are cool and so crisp it's like they've been ironed. I lie down, close my eyes, and walk myself through recipes. Is it 300 or 350 grams of butter in Swiss meringue buttercream? I twist my ring. 350. Definitely. And don't forget to sieve the pastry cr—My phone pings.

> We're crossing the bridge! Dad says our ETA is 20 minutes!!!!!!!!!!!

I can't even count the number of exclamation points after the last sentence. I text back.

> Call me when you get here.

I roll off the bed to scare up that information sheet. Right after "Any Questions?" there's a phone number, which I punch in before I can chicken out. A nice lady answers and says of course my friends are welcome at the pizza party and is there anything I need? When I say no, she signs off with "Cheerio."

I've got twenty sweet minutes to spend prone on that

comfy mattress. Dr. Lee predicted the exhaustion would taper off after the first few infusions, but she said every body is different. My decidedly different body chooses to stay tired.

It's too much effort to flip off the lights and close the drapes so I plop one of the pillows over my eyes. My brain is a blank whiteboard for a few minutes before the Dad memories appear. I roll the dandelion ring around and around on my finger, making wishes that can never come true: *I wish you were here. For the bake-off. For everything.* Above the notes of Lysol and bleach, I catch a whiff of Doublemint. One of these days, the memories will arrive sans the side of tears. But truthfully, tears are a small price to pay for a moment with Dad. What was that song lyric Elly told me about? The cracks in our heart let the light through? I place my hand on my chest. Lots of chances for light.

My phone buzzes and Elly's screaming in my ear. "We're here! In the lobby!"

"Be right down!"

As soon as the elevator door opens, I'm smooshed in a bear hug.

"Tess!" Elly lifts me off the ground.

"Don't break her. She's got to bake tomorrow!" Raj tugs Elly loose and gives me a gentler hug. "Hey, friend. How are you doing?"

"Aside from having the wind knocked out of me, peachy keen."

"I brought you this." Wayne holds out a card. "Everyone in homeroom signed it."

All kinds of messages are scrawled on the inside, but one jumps out at me: *You've got this, Ms. Bread Science. Love, Emmett and Ruffles.* "This is super special. Thanks." I hug Wayne and bend down to scratch behind Rexi's ears, hiding my smile.

"Nervous?" Rajit asks.

Elly smacks him. "Don't put ideas in her head! Besides, what does she have to be nervous about?"

"The competition?" I suggest.

"*Pfft.*" She flaps her hand. "So what's the plan?"

I tell her.

"Grueling." She squinches her eyes. "You can handle it. Can't you?"

"Raring to go." Elly practically ties Mom in the worrywart department. Easier to fake it till I make it.

"Where's the fam?" Rajit flips through the brochure rack and pulls out a Portland Guide.

"At the pool. They'll meet us at the pizza party. You guys want to come, right?"

"Are you kidding?" Elly gives me a look. "What do you guys want to do while she's at the private shindig?"

Rajit points out a window. "Visit the Mother Ship. Powell's."

"We went there once," says Wayne. "Rexi liked it because they gave her a dog treat."

"Bookstore it is." Elly fixes my collar. "See you soon."

I putter around in my room, arranging and rearranging my clothes, until it's time to go. Too late now, but I wish I'd packed my denim jacket. I feel together when I wear it. Definitely in need of a power wardrobe right now.

The room clock flashes five. I watch it for another couple minutes before I head out. I do not want to be early.

"Tess!" Chef Marie breaks away from a knot of people when she sees me. "Oh, so glad you're here."

"Me too." At the competition. Not so much at this reception. I'm not really a chit-chatter.

"You remember Maren? And Simon?" She waves two kids over and we all say hi. "I'll be right back. Talk amongst yourselves." Chef Marie floats away to corner a guy in a navy blazer.

"Look at us. A regular Three Musketeers. The only ones who came back from our year," says Simon.

"Have you guys done any other competitions since?" Maren grabs two sodas from a passing waiter. I shake my head no thanks when she offers me one.

Simon takes it. "Dying for caffeine. I entered a pie in the state fair." He guzzles his Coke. "Blue ribbon." There's nothing braggy in his tone.

"Congrats," I say.

Maren wrinkles her nose. "I tried out for *Frosted Junior*. Twice. Didn't even get invited to the in-person audition."

"Wow. I'm shocked." And I am. She was my pick to win three years ago. Her Sachertorte was about ten steps above my ability.

"Yeah. Well." She wraps a napkin around the icy glass.

I don't really want to cover the ground since our last meeting so I change the subject. "What do you think our first bake will be?"

"Rumor is that it's going to involve graham crackers." Simon crunches an ice cube.

"Seriously? Kind of basic, isn't it?" Maren sounds surprised.

"Like I said. A rumor." Simon takes in the room. "You guys want a snack? I'm starved."

I shake my head.

"Go for it," Maren says. "We'll hang here."

We watch Simon slowly circle the appetizer table. Evidently, the options are fascinating.

Maren breaks away to glance at me. "I'm sorry I never even sent you a card after. I mean, I didn't know your address, but still—"

"That's okay." I find it hard to breathe. It was probably too much to hope that this wouldn't come up. "Do you care if we don't talk about it?"

"Sorry. Sorry. But I wanted you to know."

Simon returns, carrying a paper plate piled with pretzels.

I can't help it. "All that good stuff over there and you pick pretzels?"

He grins. "What can I say? I'm a sucker for crunchy carbs."

Maren elbows me. "That's her. Flora Welch. She made it to the semis twice in *Frosted Junior*." She snags a handful of Simon's pretzels.

"How do we compete with her blackberry brioche bread pudding?" Simon's raised eyebrows bump against his bangs.

I channel my inner Elly for a pep talk. "Says the guy who killed it last time with that chocolate éclair cake and your mascarpone tart with the thyme shortbread crust." I direct the last to Maren.

"That cake *was* killer." Simon cocks his head, grins.

Maren flexes her biceps. "Call me Super Baker!"

"Hold that pose." I take her picture.

"Selfies!" Maren grabs my phone and herds us all together.

Across the room, a mic screeches with feedback. Since my hands are empty, I can cover my ears. Maren and Simon hunch up their shoulders, groaning.

"Now that I have your attention!" Chef Marie laughs off the techno glitch. "I'm delighted to welcome you to our tenth-anniversary bake-off. Before I go over the agenda and housekeeping details, please welcome Jubilee Flour's representative and guest judge, Mr. Kenton. He'll help us with the final round on Sunday." She motions the guy in the blazer over to the podium. Mr. Kenton says how excited he is to be here and tries out a baking joke, which is a total flop. But Maren, Simon, and I laugh politely. Then he turns it back to Chef Marie.

"And now I want you to meet each other. Please stand when I call your name. Max Bentwood, Harley Duncan, Alpana Jain, Tess Medina"—my stomach flips—"Simon Nguyen, Maren Taylor, Flora Welch, Ping Wong." When the clapping dies down, Chef Marie goes over the schedule and other basics. She ends with, "Oh, and the most important rule of all: Have fun!"

At that, the ballroom doors open and families flood in. "Tessie!" Gracie hurtles toward me, a chlorine-scented cyclone, and grabs my legs. "This is my sister," she tells Maren and Simon.

"I never would've guessed," Maren teases.

"Pizza is served!" Simon beelines for the buffet table.

"See you in the morning, Tess." Maren joins her family.

"Mom and Scott are over here." Gracie tugs me across the room.

Mom puts her coat and purse on some chairs. "Saving spots for the rest of Team Tess."

"Don't forget Rexi!" Gracie says.

"They might be a while. They went to Powell's." I pull out a chair and sit down, suddenly so weary. Small talk wears me out.

Mr. Liu arrives a little later. "Elly texted that they'll be here in about ten minutes," he tells me.

"You guys go ahead and get food. I'll wait." I'm not sure what I'm going to eat; pizza is sure to get the Knife riled up.

A few minutes later, my crew appears, lugging handled paper sacks. "You will not believe the bargains we scored!" Rajit collapses on a chair.

"Rexi got treats." Wayne signals her into a down under the table. "And I got a book on football. I might give it to Emmett for his birthday. Or I might keep it."

"You could lend it to him," I suggest.

"Good idea!" Wayne hangs his jacket on the back of his chair.

Elly digs around in the bottom of her sack. "Ta-dah!" She presents me with a couple old kids' books, *Owl at Home* and *Owl Babies*.

"That's so sweet." I'm sure Rajit and Wayne are confused; they don't know about Owlie.

"Who else is starving?" Elly leads the way over to the buffet table. Pretty much pizza, pizza, or pizza. Rajit and Wayne pile slices up on their plates. I take a small plain cheese, grateful that Mom packed snacks.

"So have you checked out the competition?" Elly slides two veggie slices onto her plate.

"Not really. I mostly talked with the kids I knew from before. Maren and Simon." I point them out.

"Trash talking?" Elly asks.

I laugh. "Not quite."

"That girl looks familiar." Rajit gestures down the long buffet.

"That's Flora Welch. She made it to the semis on *Frosted Junior*. Twice." Wayne grabs a breadstick.

"I didn't know you watched baking shows!" I add carrot and celery sticks to my plate.

"Only since we became friends."

His answer blurs my eyes. "Hey, thanks, Wayne."

"Want me to trip her?" Elly grins diabolically.

I jab her in the side. "You nut."

She tosses her hair. "All's fair in love and baking."

Back at the table, Gracie tells joke after four-year-old joke, encouraged by Elly's laughter. Mr. Liu shows her a magic trick with a quarter. She is the complete center of attention, which is fine with me. I don't remember being this nervous last time.

But last time was before the Knife.

Chapter 23

"Breakfast!" Mom calls through the privacy door.

I open it to find her holding out a fancy tray.

"For me?"

"Just for you." She sets it on the desk.

I lift the silver cover. Berries, toast, scrambled eggs. And a steaming cup of herbal tea. "This is perfect."

"Okay if we catch up with you at the first round?" She brushes my hair back over my shoulder. "We're going to try to wear Gracie out at the pool again after we eat."

"Sounds good." I'm buttering toast when my phone pings.

At Voodoo Doughnuts. Want anything?

A sprinkle one for Gracie.

Roger that.

I got room service!

I text Elly a picture of my tray.

Classy. How U doing?

I pause before replying. Mentally scan my gut.

Doing. Kinda nervous.

You've got this!

Rajit sends a GIF of smoke pouring out of an oven.

With friends like you . . .

I reply.

He's hilarious,

Elly texts.

You should eat before it gets cold.

k. See u soon?

Front row seats!

I brush my teeth twice after breakfast. Change my clothes three times. Nothing looks right. Or feels right. I can't even get my ID lanyard on straight.

The room phone rings and I shriek. *Get a grip. In four. Out eight.* "Hello?"

"Good morning, Miss Medina. Calling to remind you to be in Ballroom B in fifteen minutes."

Stinging ice pellets of adrenaline shoot through me. "Th-thanks." I hang up and press my hands to my chest to prevent my heart from jumping right through my ribs. It's go time. This outfit will have to do. Deep breaths. No fainting allowed.

Too antsy to wait for the elevator, I take the stairs. The eight flights down chase off some of the butterflies; my hands are almost steady when I enter the ballroom.

Eight workstations, each with an oven, are staggered up front. Five commercial refrigerators ring the stage area. A guy with a clipboard darts around a delivery person wheeling in a dolly stacked with flour sacks, and when I try to get out of the way of a lady carrying a stack of aprons, I step on someone's toes.

"Oh, so sorry." I turn around.

Flora Welch lifts her Doc Martened right foot. "No harm done."

I introduce myself.

"I can read."

Burn. "Oh, I forgot about the name tag." She's not wearing hers.

"What's your specialty bake?"

I shrug. "Probably cupcakes. But my macarons always have nice feet."

Flora sniffs. "I'm known for my cheesecake baklava. With homemade phyllo."

If she's trying to psych me out, it's working. *In four. Out eight.* "That sounds delicious. Perfect for spring."

"Yes, it is." She struts away.

"Ready to rock?" Simon appears, tying on a Jubilee Flour apron.

I regroup. "Gotta grab one of those"—I point to the apron—"and check out my station."

"May your cookies never crumble!"

"Back at you." We fist bump and I grab an apron and head to the station where my name's spelled out in huge blue letters that match the Jubilee Flour logo. I take a selfie and send it to Elly, who shoots back:

> You're going to be impossible to live with now.

The last of the Flora ick melts away and I'm almost breathing normally.

My phone buzzes with another text.

Be there asap. Not letting us in yet.

I send a thumbs-up before tying my apron.

The long worktable is fitted out with lower shelves underneath stacked with gleaming cookie sheets, muffin tins, fluted tart pans, and cake pans—square, round, and rectangular. A bouquet of spatulas, wooden spoons, and whisks fills a tool jar resting on the stainless steel tabletop, next to a butcher block cutting board and canisters of flour, and white, brown, and powdered sugar. We each have our own stand mixer; mine's Blue Willow. I know because I almost chose that color instead of Bernice. I check the fit of the beater and run through the speeds, trying to ignore the blip in my stomach at the sight of all those empty chairs. Chairs that will soon be filled with people watching us. Watching me.

Who needs Flora? I'm doing a great job of psyching myself out. Like a couple of the other contestants, I scope out the gas range and cooktop combos, convection ovens, the blast chiller, and half a dozen stainless steel racks serving as a pantry.

"Edible diamond dust! I've died and gone to heaven." Maren's at my shoulder. "Oh man. Sorry. I didn't mean—"

"It's okay." And it is. "This is amazing." The shelf in front of me has four types of cinnamon: Indonesian, Saigon,

Vietnamese, and Ceylon, which is a budget buster but utterly transforms a pumpkin pie. "Can you imagine the grocery bill?"

"Oh, look!" Maren snags a container of silver heart-shaped dragées. "I'm going to figure out a way to use these, for sure."

A container of marzipan flowers catches my eye. They'd be fun; maybe on a tart?

"Contestants, please listen up." A tall woman waves a clipboard to get our attention. "Five minutes till we let guests in. Please follow Finn to the green room for your grand entrance." Finn waves their hand and we tumble after like baby ducks.

"A grand entrance?" I mumble. "Like we're not nervous enough already?"

"I hear you." Harley straightens his bow tie. "I hope I don't hurl."

"So do we!" Simon says. Alpana and Ping laugh uneasily.

"Deep breaths. No one's going to hurl." Maren radiates such confidence I believe her.

Every minute, Finn calls out how much time is left. At three minutes, Harley moans.

Maren hands him a ginger candy. "Chew this. It'll help."

"Two minutes," Finn says. "And remember, you'll go out in alpha order."

Harley pops the candy into his mouth. I'm tempted to

ask Maren if she has any spares. I can totally relate to Harley's squirrelly innards.

"One." Finn taps their earbuds, listening.

Suddenly, I need to pee.

"Ready?" Finn holds up both hands, then points at Max. "Go!"

Max sucks in a breath and strides through the door. After a few beats, Finn waves Harley through, and then the rest of us in turn. I am once again thankful for a last name that keeps me smack in the middle, rarely first or last.

I walk into a wall of noise. Everyone's cheering and shouting, but the sound of my name rises above the racket. Elly's bouncing up and down. Oh my frog. Is that a pompom she's waving? She promised! Gracie's standing on her chair, with her own pom-pom, waving back and forth like the Noodley Men she loves. Mom's tugging her to sit. I blow them a kiss.

"Are we ready to bake?" Chef Marie shouts, and the crowd shouts back, "Yes!" Ha! Chef Marie should be asking us contestants.

Max and Simon blow up a fist bump, Flora does a parade princess wave, and I straighten my apron.

"The next two days will be jam-packed with surprises. And here is our first." Chef Marie motions to the back of the room and a familiar figure starts down the center aisle.

It can't be. I grip the edge of the worktable to keep myself upright.

"Oh. My. Gosh." Not even Flora can keep her cool at the sight of that unmistakable handlebar mustache.

"Contestants, allow me to introduce my fellow judge for this competition. Deke Friedman, owner of City of Angels Cakes and host of the Food Channel's *Frosted Junior*!"

People jump to their feet, screaming. Deke waves his tattoo-sleeved arms as he powers to the front of the room. His bald head's even shinier in person. If someone asked me my name right now, I would not be able to answer. I am in the same room with Deke Friedman. Simon wears an ear-to-ear grin; Harley's as white as baking soda.

"Happy to see you again, Marie. What's cooking?"

"Glad you asked." She hands him a manila folder. "Here's the first challenge. Ready to get things rolling?"

The audience groans at her attempted joke.

"You bet." Deke pulls an oversized recipe card out of the envelope and reads, "The first challenge is to make fake-out versions of takeout. Your task is to create a sweet treat that looks like a classic savory food in ninety minutes."

"I call pizza," Flora blurts out.

"Eager beaver." Chef Marie smiles sympathetically, then pulls eight square blue cards from her apron pocket.

"But it's going to be luck of the draw. When I call your name, come pick a card."

Simon's first. "Sushi!" He pumps his fist.

Flora's next. "Got what I wanted." She shows the card. Pizza.

Chef Marie keeps calling names. I'm dead last.

Tacos.

Deke sweeps his arm up like a starting flag. "Okay. Your ninety minutes starts . . . NOW!"

"Go, Tess, go!" Elly's voice soars over the audience noise and the sounds of my seven competitors scrambling to assemble ingredients. I drop the taco card on my workstation and grab a piece of paper. Dad always made a plan. To get my brain juices flowing, I draw a taco on the paper. It's like I've never seen or eaten one before. Get a grip. Think! *In four. Out eight.* Crumbled brownie crumbs sort of look like ground meat. Maybe dye coconut flakes for lettuce and thinly slice some Circus Peanut candies to resemble grated cheese. But how to replicate that crunchy taco shell?

I look over and Flora's already got a batch of cookie dough going for her pizza crust. Simon's working green and brown food coloring into fondant: sweet seaweed. Clever. Harley's making pâte à choux for faux bagels. And Maren's weighing out flour.

Deke stops at my station. "What's your plan?" he asks.

I stammer as I tell him what I've come up with so far.

"Taco shell?" he asks.

"To be determined." Doomed before I even start.

"I'll leave you to it." He pats my mixer and moves away to check on someone else.

I take a swig from my water bottle. Take a breath. Think: crunchy, crunchy, crunchy.

Flora flounces past with baskets of fruit from the pantry shelves. Something shiny behind her catches my eye. I grab the pizzelle iron before anyone else does. Italian waffle cookies are usually crisp and flat, but maybe I could form them into taco shells? Worth a try.

"Time?" Max calls.

"Fifteen minutes gone," Finn answers.

Time to kick it up a notch, as Emeril would say. I whip up the brownies, using my trio of secret weapons: espresso powder, water in the eggs, and 50 grams of powdered sugar with the granulated. I slide the pan into the oven and snag the canister of coconut flakes.

"Anybody got the cocoa powder?" Harley calls out.

I wave splotchy green hands. "Over here."

"Are you done with it?" He hesitates.

I hit the faucet and lather up with soap. "Yep. All yours." Green soapy water swirls down the drain, but my hands still look grass-stained.

Deke bangs a metal spoon on a bundt pan. "Bakers! Your attention, please."

I stop in mid-scrub. *Frosted Junior* is full of surprises for its contestants; did Deke bring that to this competition? My question is answered in seconds.

"We don't want your fake-out food to feel lonely. So, we're asking you to also create an accompaniment."

Harley groans. Maren emits a mousy squeak.

"There's only an hour left." Simon sounds stunned.

We should've expected something like this the minute we saw Deke. Shenanigans are part of his persona, like that mustache.

Only one thing goes with tacos: salsa. If I'm going to edge out the Fabulous Flora, a single salsa won't do. I'll make red *and* green. A quick visit to the pantry reveals perfectly ripe early season strawberries—a passable stand-in for tomatoes and even tastier with mint, lemon zest, and a pinch of sugar. I toss those into my basket and add kiwis as stand-ins for tomatillos in the green salsa, which will be yummy with tiny pineapple bits for onions and a squeeze of lime. Two cheery ceramic bowls look like perfect salsa-serving dishes so I snag those, too, and hustle back to my station as the timer for the brownies is going off.

"Those smell great." Chef Marie stops by my workstation. "How are you using them?"

"For the ground beef."

She nods. "Fun idea. Carry on."

I run the brownies to the blast chiller then race back to my station to chop strawberries.

"Thirty minutes!" Finn hollers.

Simon loses his cool.

"What's wrong?" I call over.

He holds up a cookie sheet with sugar cookies as dark as his hair. "I was going to crumble these to make fake miso soup to go with my sushi." He dumps the burnt cookies in the trash. "Now what am I going to do?"

I'm not a sushi fan myself, but Scott is. "How about edamame, out of green fondant?"

Simon shakes his head. "Already used fondant for the seaweed."

I toss the minced mint with the strawberries. "Marzipan?"

"My hero!" He dashes to the pantry, and I dash over to the blast chiller to grab my brownies. They're cool enough to whisk up into uneven chunks so they'll look more like browned ground beef. The clock's ticking and I've still got to make my pizzelles, the green salsa, and then plate everything.

After a quick wipe down of my station, I start the pizzelles. When a few drops of water sizzle on the iron, it's ready for batter. I pour it in and count out thirty seconds. Then I take a sniff. Is it done? Ten more seconds and I lift the lid.

Hockey puck. I take a nibble. Deliciously vanilla hockey puck but still a hockey puck. I wipe off the iron, respray with oil, and try again. At thirty seconds, I pull off the pizzelle and drape it over a wooden spoon handle to form the first taco shell. Street tacos usually come in threes so that means making five more. While the shells cool, I chop up kiwi and pineapple, and drizzle in fresh lime juice.

Finn bangs on a pot with a metal spoon. "One minute, bakers!"

Oh my frog. I haven't begun to plate anything. I reach for the two bowls I'd snagged. Weren't they on the countertop?

"Lose something?" Simon asks.

"Salsa bowls." They aren't under the tea towel. Or by the brownie pan. No time to keep looking. I make a snap decision to use small glass prep bowls instead and then arrange the tacos on a red-checked- paper food tray. Not what I envisioned but sometimes it's about progress not perfection. A couple mint leaves to garnish the salsas and, voilà. Finished.

"Hands up!" Finn calls out. "Back away from your bakes."

Still holding some mint leaves, I shoot my hands above my head.

"You survived your first round!" Deke claps as he takes

a seat behind a high table. "We can't wait to see what you've prepared."

"Harley? Do you mind starting?" Chef Marie takes a seat next to Deke.

Harley's face is as pale as his faux bagels. Not a good look for either.

Chef Marie smiles in encouragement. "Tell us about your fake-out dish."

Harley gestures with a shaky hand. "Those are pâte à choux bagels with lox; I thin-sliced a dyed peach half to make the lox."

"Clever." Chef Marie's compliment restores some color to Harley's face.

"And what's the side?" Deke asks.

"A latte?"

Deke raises his eyebrows. "You don't sound sure about that, man."

My throat tightens in empathy. Poor Harley.

"It didn't turn out the way I imagined." Harley tugs at his bow tie. "It's an espresso cupcake topped with meringue to look like foam."

Deke hands Chef Marie a fork. "Time to taste?"

They praise Harley's pâte à choux and the flavor of the cupcake. "But the bagel's pretty pale, and even though the cupcake has lovely flavor—"

"So moist," Chef Marie interjects.

"Your side doesn't look like a latte. It looks like a cupcake." Deke puts down his fork.

Harley swallows so hard I can see his Adam's apple sliding up and down. The judging's tougher than it was when we were little kids.

"Thanks, man," Deke says.

Dismissed, Harley collapses on a chair by the pantry.

Maren's sliders with apple "fries" are a hit. Chef Marie asks for the recipe. Simon's sushi seaweed is a startling bright green—"a bit off-putting," says Deke—but he gets raves for his marzipan edamame. Simon whispers, "Thanks" as he passes me to sit with the others. Deke eats two of Max's cake-pop corn dogs but dings him on the graham cracker–coated Red Vine "onion rings" because they're hard to chew. Alpana wows Chef Marie with her pot stickers and homemade chocolate caramel "plum" sauce, and Ping gets a fist bump from Deke for her spaghetti and meatballs. "This looks like a bowl of the real thing," Chef Marie tells her. And it does. I wonder if I can sneak out the back.

"Flora?" Chef Marie arranges her notepad in front of her. "Would you present your fake-out?"

Flora sets her creation in front of the judges. "Pizza with bread sticks and marinara sauce," she announces. The marinara sauce is served in a pair of cheery ceramic bowls. *My* cheery bowls. I can't believe she'd stoop that low. "The bread sticks are made with my grandma's favorite biscotti recipe; I added a touch of cardamom to compliment the strawberry chutney."

My brain shuts down and I don't even hear what Chef Marie and Deke say next. The stress is whipping my stomach juices into a vinegary froth. I squeeze my eyes, willing those juices to stay inside my body.

"And, Tess, what do you have for us?" Chef Marie's smile is a lifeline.

I swallow hard. "Street tacos with two types of salsa."

Deke picks up one of the tacos, looks it over, then crunches into it. "This is like eating the real thing. What did you end up doing for the shells? Pizzelles?"

I nod.

He takes a second bite! "That's a nice moist brownie."

Chef Marie samples the red salsa. "This is delicious. Love the mint."

Deke makes a face after tasting.

"I gotta disagree. The mint overwhelms the berries." He reaches for the green salsa. "I like the brightness of this one, though."

"Thank you, Tess." Chef Marie picks up her pen.

I find a chair and sit. Elly's flapping her hands in the air, mouthing, "You did it!" Rajit gives me double thumbs-up. Wayne's got Rexi on his lap and is waving her front paws. Scott's arm is around Mom's shoulder; their grins are bright enough to land a plane. Gracie's shaking the stuffing out of her Barbie pom-poms. They have no clue that I blew it. Too much mint. Why didn't I remember? Deke hates mint.

"This is going to be tough." Chef Marie looks genuinely sad about having to vote someone off the island. I can't get a read on Deke. "Excuse us; we'll be back in ten minutes with our announcement."

All eight of us exhale in one huge tidal wave breath. Finn rolls out a tray of water bottles. "Help yourself," they say.

"Can we talk to our families?" Harley asks.

"Go for it."

I grab a bottle of water. Elly meets me halfway to crunch me in a hug.

"A. Mazing." She lets go. "Even from here, that taco looked like the real thing."

"Mint." I struggle to open the water bottle. Wayne takes it from me.

"An herb," Rajit says.

Wayne hands the opened bottle back.

I take a sip. "Supremely helpful," I tell Rajit. "How could I forget Deke detests mint?"

Elly waves the thought away. "That's his prob. Chef Marie loved it."

They're my friends. Required to cheer me up.

"How are you?" Mom tags me with her parent-ray.

Another sip. "It's hot up there. The ovens and all." If I

give even one hint that I don't feel well, she'll freak. I hold up the water bottle. "This helps."

She nods, but I can tell I haven't convinced her.

"You're the best baker!" Gracie gloms on to me; I pat her back before gently peeling her off.

Elly swings Gracie's hands and they spin in circles. "Hollywood, here we come!"

I cover my ears. "Did you see Ping's spaghetti? And Deke ate two of Max's corn dogs! Two!"

Scott leans in and whispers, "It'll all be okay in the end. And if it's not okay, it's not the end." He wraps his arm around my shoulder and squeezes. I lean in, trying to soak up some of his calm. His strength. And I catch a whiff of Doublemint. *Thanks, Dad.*

I nibble the granola bar Mom forces on me, which soaks up some of the sour in that vinegar pit. Everyone fulfills their duty to prop me up. I nod and pretend all the kind things they're saying are true.

A door at the back pops open; Deke holds it while Chef Marie steps through. I whimper.

"You've got this." Rajit pats my back.

"Team Tess!" Elly moonwalks.

"Yeah. Team Tess!" Wayne copies Elly.

"No matter what, you're a winner in our book." Mom kisses my cheek.

Oh my frog. They're killing me.

Finn maneuvers us into a semi-straight line facing Chef Marie and Deke. Maren grabs my hand. Harley's bow tie is askew. Simon worries a thread on his apron pocket; Alpana chews a thumbnail. Even Flora's smile wobbles at the edges. Why did I think this bake-off was a good idea?

Chef Marie starts talking. Blah blah blah. Then Deke talks. Blah blah blah. I can see their mouths moving. But apparently nothing's coming out. Maren murmurs something. "It'll be okay," I whisper, taking a deep breath. In four. Out eight. *Get a grip.*

"We gave you a tough challenge and, though it got even tougher partway through, you all rose to the occasion." Chef Marie fiddles with the top button of her chef's jacket. "This was an extremely difficult decision."

"Totally." Deke's head bobs in agreement. "But two bakers really wowed us. Flora and Ping, you will advance to the next round."

"Go, Flora!" someone calls out.

"Dad." Flora rolls her eyes. As if having a dad is embarrassing.

"You deserve it," I say to Ping, who's on my other side. I nod down the line at Flora.

"Please remember that you got here because you are terrific bakers. Among the best." Chef Marie's eyes glitter. Are those tears?

I'm out. I know it.

"We drew straws and I lost. That means I have to deliver the bad news." Deke strokes his mustache. "Simon? Harley? Sorry, dudes. You won't be moving on."

I glance over. Harley's tie is completely sidewise and Simon's smile slides off his face. I feel terrible.

And relieved.

I am such a jerk.

Deke shakes their hands. Chef Marie hugs. "Keep baking," she encourages.

Finn calls for a short break. Harley and Simon disappear for a bit but reemerge from wherever as the buzzer sounds to start the next round. Harley's tie is gone and his eyes look red, even from where I'm standing. Simon's leaning against his mom, eating a sandwich.

"Round two!" Finn snaps a clapperboard. "To your stations."

I glance at Harley and Simon. I know they're completely bummed.

But I bet their stomachs are no longer churning.

Chapter 24

Despite announcing, "I don't do pies," Maren's poached-peach sour cream caramel creation was stunning. Alpana stole the show with a chai pie that made my mouth water. My macaroon cherry wasn't too shabby, either—I followed Dad's rule and kept everything chilled, flour included. Chef Marie kept nibbling at the crust after her test bite, as good as winning gold at the Olympics. Of course, Flora created a perfect plum-blueberry galette, glistening with demerara sugar. At the end of round two, there were only four of us; Ping forgot to vent her pie, and Max's lemon curd was soup.

Elly waves a stack of paper plates. "Life is short; eat dessert first!" We gather on stuffed chairs around a big table on the landing near the elevator, and Mom starts handing the remaining slices of my pie around. I shake my head at the one she offers me.

"Nerves?" she asks.

"Yeah." It's not a complete fib. "This was harder than I thought. I'm solid with the basics, but Flora and her fancy stuff—"

"You do you," Elly butts in, licking filling off her thumb. "This is delicious."

"Scrumptious," Rajit adds. "I mean, scrummy."

"I could eat the whole thing," says Wayne.

"You are unreliable sources." I sip my water.

"Not us." Elly forks up another bite.

"No way." Rajit tosses his empty paper plate.

"Are you done with that?" Wayne eyes Gracie's piece, which she hands over.

Mr. Liu picks up a crumb of crust left in the pie pan. "The only thing wrong with this pie is that it's all gone!" Conversations swirl around me, but I can't focus. My body is so wiped it's melting into the chair. Not sure I'll ever get up.

"Earth calling Tess." Rajit pokes me. "We're all going to the pool before dinner. Coming?"

"Cannonball!" Wayne says.

"You can borrow my mermaid flippers," Gracie tells Elly.

I now know where that expression "bone tired" comes from. I swear every part of me is yawning. "I think I'll take a catnap. Long day."

Mom hugs me. "Smart idea."

The adults and Gracie hang around chatting while the rest of us head up in the elevator.

"So that Flora. Is she your biggest competition?" Elly pushes the button for our floor.

"I've never even heard of a galette before." Rajit checks himself out in the gleam of the decorative brass plates.

"She baked it in season nine of *Frosted Junior*," Wayne says. "But with a different kind of fruit. Maybe pears?"

"I don't have her baking chops." I yawn.

"We boring you?" Elly elbows me.

"Ha ha."

"She better watch out," Rajit says.

"I wish."

"Rexi loved your pie," says Wayne. "And she is very picky."

We file out when the doors open. "See you guys at dinner."

I unlock my room, slip out of my clothes, and fall face-first on the freshly made bed. *Must. Have. Sleep.* The pillowcase is deliciously cool against my cheek, the sheets deliciously cool against my bare legs. The ovens and the lights and the running around got me overheated. That's all. I flop on my side to reach for the water bottle. I didn't drink enough; that's why I'm so out of it. I remember the rest of Dad's advice about pie baking— keep everything chilled, even the baker—and take a swig. Icy water hits my stomach like hailstones. I rub my middle to calm things down, then curl up, close my eyes, and drift off.

*   *   *

The scritch-scratch in my gut wakes me. I peel the sheets away, and ease myself up, slowly, slowly, slowly, so I don't annoy the Knife. My phone pings.

> Are u coming down?

Oh my frog. It's after six.

> On my way!

I reply. But I don't want to be on my way. I want to crawl back in bed, save up my energy, keep the Knife quiet. I get a grip and talk myself through the rest of the steps to get ready: zip on jeans, wash face, brush hair. Before I grab the doorknob, I check in with my gut. Maybe I was dreaming before; everything seems okay now.

My friends are clumped together, damp-haired, at the far end of the table.

"You missed a wild game of Marco Polo," Elly says.

"A little too wild." Rajit pulls up his shirtsleeve to show off a bruise. "Elly's a brute."

"It was an accident, wasn't it, Gracie?"

"Yep!" Gracie would agree with anything Elly says.

"They wouldn't let Rexi swim," Wayne says sadly. "But your mom watched her so I could. Gracie and I had a race."

"And I won!" Gracie hops around in her chair.

I smile my thanks at Wayne.

The waiter works his way around the table to take my order. "Spaghetti, please, with the sauce on the side."

Mom's too far away to comment, but Scott gives me a look. "Nerves," I mouth.

Sometimes I wish we could control people like we do virtual assistants. Then I could say, "Elly, reduce volume and enthusiasm by fifty percent." Or: "Gracie, stop jumping up and down." Or: "Mom, enough with the worried looks already."

Elly grabs the paper napkin that came with Rajit's Dr Pepper, writes something down, and hands it to me. "Put this in your apron for tomorrow."

Everyone's talking, but all I can do is pick at my noodles. After a while, the waiter brings dessert menus and puts them in the middle of the table.

Rajit grabs one. "I know we already had dessert, but—"

"We swam. We deserve it!" Elly reads over his shoulder. "Oh, I'm having an ice cream sundae!"

"Lava cake for me," says Wayne. "How about you, Tess?"

I press my fingers to my mouth. "I spent the day up to my eyebrows in sugar. I'll pass." I toss a napkin over my plate to hide how much spaghetti is left.

Gracie's head rests on the table. "Someone's hit the wall." Mom scoots her chair back.

I hop up. "You haven't finished your coffee. I'll get her ready for bed."

"Don't you want to hang with us?" Elly's lower lip pokes out.

"We start earlier tomorrow. I need to crash."

Elly leans back as the waiter places a sundae in front of her. "I totally get it. Forty winks and you'll be ready to roll."

After good nights all around, I take Gracie's sticky hand. When we get out at our floor, she stretches out her arms. "Carry me." Her head bobs on my shoulder as I walk the long hall toward Mom and Scott's room. She stirs when I open the door, then starts to cry. I know better than to push teeth brushing, so I give it a pass and wrestle her into a nightie and bed.

She cuddles Mr. Monkey. "Tell me a story."

I pull the covers over her shoulder. "A short one, okay? I'm beat."

"Tell me about the Joyful Cookies?" She rubs Mr. Monkey's tail against her cheek.

"You remember that one?" Maybe she hasn't completely forgotten Dad.

"The lady yelled, but Dad didn't yell back."

"Yep." I tell her the whole story. "He was a really good guy."

"You should bake some of those cookies. For the contest." She yawns.

"Not fancy enough. But how about if the two of us make a batch when we get home?"

The pillowcase rustles as she nods. "Night, Tessie."

"Night, Gracie." I kiss her forehead and tiptoe to my room, leaving the privacy door ajar so I can listen for her.

I brush my teeth. What a coincidence that Gracie would ask for that story, out of the blue. I spit, then catch myself in the mirror. Smile. Maybe not such a coincidence. *Thanks, Dad.*

I flip the switch, touch my ring, and make a wish.

Alpana and Maren are already in the green room when I arrive. Finn hands me a fresh apron. "Doing okay?" they ask.

"Nervous," I confess.

"Oh, me too." Alpana holds up her hands. "No fingernails left."

"I devoured an entire pint of Ben & Jerry's last night," Maren confesses.

"You're all doing great. Don't forget to celebrate the fact that you've made it this far," Finn says.

"Can you tell us anything about what to expect today?" Maren asks.

"Sorry." Finn signs zipping lips. "Trust me: It'll be fun."

"What'll be fun?" Flora breezes in carrying a paper coffee cup. I can't imagine adding caffeine to my body; my nerves would spontaneously combust.

"Today." Finn hands Flora an apron. "Anybody need anything?"

"Another stomach!" Alpana paces from one side of the room to the other.

"Are you sick?" Flora asks.

"Naw. Just anxious." Alpana completes another couple loops.

I'm about ready to join her when Finn opens the door. "Deep breaths, friends. Time to head on in."

"Ack!" Alpana freezes. Maren shakes all over like a wet dog. Flora takes another sip of her coffee and tosses the cup.

"Last one there is a burned biscuit," she says.

I swipe damp palms against my apron and follow her out. Deke and Chef Marie are waiting. I look for my family and friends, and when I see them, the jangling inside me quiets. My shoulders unknot. I can do this. I am doing this. I am an experienced baker. It's in my genes.

Chef Marie welcomes the audience and then turns to us. "You overcame yesterday's challenges with grace and now you're here. Round three!"

Applause interrupts her. "Absolutely," she says. "Let's give these contestants a much-deserved hand." Someone in the crowd hollers out, "Woot-woot!" Elly.

Deke pats his mustache. "This next bake requires you to use my all-time favorite vegetable—"

"What?" Alpana blurts out.

"Chocolate!" He cackles. "Now, chocolate may seem simple, but remember. You need to wow us to make it to the final round. And you've got two hours to do it."

Chef Marie holds up the timer. "Ready, set, bake!"

Deke's a chocoholic so this chocolate challenge is no surprise. I'd played around with one of Dad's mousse recipes and created a s'mores version that Elly goes bonkers over. It's perfect for filling a dark chocolate cake covered with chocolate ganache. Not sure about the decorations; hopefully, inspiration will come as I work.

I head over to the pantry for cake pans; Maren's beat me so I need to wait while she makes her choices.

"There've got to be tart pans." She rummages through a stack of metal pans.

"There's one." I point it out.

"You're a lifesaver!" She jogs back to her workstation.

Multilayers should impress Deke, so I pull out four round cake pans.

"I need two ten-inch rounds." Flora rushes up. "Are there any left?" She answers her own question and snags them.

Alpana's right behind her. "I hope you're okay with square pans," I say because that's all that's left.

"I'll make it work. Necessity is the mother of invention, right?" She hurries to her station, leaving me standing there while the rest get to work.

Time for me to do the same. I butter and flour the pans

then mix up the batter using sour cream, buttermilk, and espresso powder, Dad's tricks for a moist flavor-packed cake. When I lift the glass bowl off the stand mixer to scoop the batter into the cake pans, something tweaks in my gut. An unwelcome and familiar tweak. No. No! I keep moving, banging the pans on the countertop to release the air bubbles. Slide them into the oven. Set the timer.

Heat spreads from my middle, up to my head, down to my feet; sweat trickles down my spine. The whisk wobbles as I mix the egg yolks, sugar, and salt to start the mousse. The air is so heavy with sugar it's hard to breathe. The Knife flicks out an exploratory blade. This cannot be happening. Not now.

"You okay?" Maren pauses on her way to the blast chiller. "Your face is all red."

I grab my water bottle. "Yeah. Fine. Just hot."

"Hard not to be with all these ovens going." Maren's forehead wrinkles. "Let me know if I can help."

"Maren to the rescue!" I force a smile because she deserves it; she would probably help Flora. After measuring heavy cream into a saucepan, I turn the flame on low, exhaling in small quiet puffs to calm the pulsing in my gut. When the cream's simmered for a bit, I whisk a quarter cup at a time into the eggs, slowly, so they don't curdle. Each flick of my wrist is matched by a flick of a Knife blade, but I manage to hold on until I get the vanilla paste added.

"Bathroom break." I hustle by Finn, holding back tears along with everything else. I sit on the toilet for an eternity, praying this is a fluke. Nerves or exhaustion or something like that. Not a flare-up.

After I wash my hands, I put a damp paper towel on the back of my neck. A small cool current travels through my shoulders, behind my ribs, into my stomach. I take a breath, do an assessment. I think I feel better. Yes. Definitely better.

"Your timer was going off, so I grabbed your cakes." Maren loosens a shell from a tart pan.

"Thank you, thank you." I would hug her, but I've got to get cracking. No pun intended. Finn's announcements of time remaining turn into white noise as I run from oven to blast chiller to workstation and back again, ticking tasks off in my head. Marshmallow mousse chilled and ready to go? Check. Warm cream poured over chocolate for the ganache? Check.

"Fifteen minutes!" This announcement pierces my fog.

"Oh my frog, I have no idea how I'll finish." I slather mousse on the bottom cake layer.

"Keep going till they yell stop." Alpana flies by with a container of peanut butter cups.

Maren's touching up the mirror glaze on her cake. "It's not over till the fat lady sings!"

The second cake layer goes on top of the s'mores mousse without cracking. Maren's glaze is dull, like she poured it on when it wasn't quite cooled. Nothing to do about it now so I don't say a word. My plan for a sleek, smooth ganache frosting job goes out the window. I bounce a spoon lightly over the icing to give it a slightly punk look.

"One minute!"

Finn's getting on my nerves. I fire up a kitchen torch and tap the cluster of mini-marshmallows topping the ganache until they're a nice golden brown. Finn's counting down the time as I shave chocolate over the top and—

"Hands up!" Finn calls.

I step away. Not photo-worthy but, considering the bathroom delay, not too bad. Dad would've put this in the pastry case, for sure. I'm not the only one who guzzles a bunch of water. Maren looks as shell-shocked as her glaze, and Alpana's about as green as the plate under her lopsided cake. Even Flora looks flustered. I catch her eye.

"This is hard." She rubs her face.

"Your cake is incredible." Where she got the time to make those chocolate ribbons, I have no idea. Can't worry about that now.

We get a fifteen-minute break while Finn sets up the judging station. I crash on the couch in the green room. Maren pushes my feet aside so she can sit. Alpana leans against the wall.

"This is tougher than a triathalon," she says. I look away when I see the tear trickle down her cheek. Give her some privacy.

Flora opens a package of cheese crackers. "What do you think they'll make us do for the final round?"

"Us?" Maren flops her head against the couch back. "I'm out. I know it."

"Did you see my cake? Leaning tower of peanut butter." Alpana accepts a cracker from Flora and munches.

"Presentation's only part of it." I try to be a cheerleader.

Alpana slides down the wall, thunking to the floor. "Let's get this over with." Her head bangs against her knees.

I'm out of cheerleader juice so I close my eyes. Finn opens the door and a breeze wafts through; I lift my hot face to the lovely cool air.

"Is it time?" Alpana doesn't lift her head.

"Here to give you the five-minute warning." Finn rests their hand on Alpana's shoulder. "You okay?"

Alpana groans. "Of course I'm not. Did you see that cake?"

"Presentation isn't—" Finn starts.

"Everything," we yell. Maren starts laughing and so do I. Pretty soon, we're all laugh-crying, even Finn. Then they tap their earpiece.

"Time to roll," they say.

"Freshen up, friends." Flora tosses face wipes around.

I tear open the package and pat my face and neck. "I feel so tropical."

That starts another round of laughter. "Laugh or you cry," Maren says. "Ready?"

"No!" Alpana's still in her seated tuck.

I nudge her with my foot. "What's the worst that can happen?"

"Everything!" She doesn't budge.

I crouch down. "We're going into the final round. The final round! Best kid bakers on the West Coast. No matter how this turns out, we can be proud."

Alpana sniffs. "You are such a Pollyanna." She takes my hand and lets me pull her to her feet. "Let's do this thing."

Everyone looks calm and collected as we await our sentences. But this time I know three other sets of legs are as wobbly as mine. Alpana's called forward first. Deke comments on the slant; Chef Marie thinks the frosting is a bit oily. "And you see this dark line here?" She points. "A sign that it's underdone. But the flavor is really wonderful."

Alpana thanks them and takes a seat. Chef Marie looks crushed to have to point out that Maren's mirror glaze is dull. "I wonder if the filling was too warm when you poured it on top?" she asks.

"I ran out of time." Maren tugs on her apron.

"Let's taste it, shall we?" Chef Marie hands Deke a fork.

"Wonderful combination of flavors," he says. "Very sophisticated."

Maren exhales.

"Maybe overbaked?" Chef Marie's nose wrinkles.

"I think so, too." But Deke takes another bite.

Maren deflates like a balloon. "Thank you."

Practically perfect Flora wows the judges with the presentation and the flavor of her elegant cake. "I taste the cinnamon and nutmeg right up front and then there's that lovely clove finish. Great balance with the chocolate."

"And so moist." Deke inspects the bite on his fork. "Absolutely delicious."

Flora rocks up and down on her toes as if she might float away.

Then me.

"Kind of digging the punk rocker icing." Deke cuts a slice. "Excellent job with the layers."

"The filling. It's a mousse, but I can't quite place . . . Oh, camping! This tastes like s'mores." Chef Marie scoops another bite.

"S'mores mousse," I say.

"Let me in there!" Deke takes a huge bite. "Now I want to sing 'Kumbaya.'"

The crowd laughs.

"Thank you, bakers, for a wonderful assortment of chocolate cakes. We'll break again for fifteen minutes and then announce the winners of this round."

No one talks in the green room. Maybe the others are doing whatever it takes not to puke, like me. Well, probably not Flora. She's got this sewn up.

The next thing I know, Finn's ushering us out front.

Chef Marie and Deke look somber. Chef Marie won't even look in my direction, which gives me my answer. She can't play favorites, but I think she wanted me to make it to the finals. Because of before.

The four of us line up on the marks Finn shows us. Maren sways and I steady her. "Just get it over with," she whispers.

I see Chef Marie's mouth moving. Words are said. But the volume's been turned off. I can't hear anything. Can't process. Then Maren hugs me. "Way to go!"

I've made it to the final round.

Me and Flora.

Scrummy.

Chapter 25

Elly raises my hand above my head. "Our champion!" She and Gracie boogie around.

"Not quite." I free my hand and untie my apron.

"*Pfft.*" Elly hands me my jacket. "Mere details. Come on. We're getting out of here. There's a food truck calling us."

"Hang on a second. We need to congratulate our ace baker, too." Mom and Scott scoop me into a group hug.

"Any guesses what our final challenge will be?" I step back and wrap my arm around Mom's waist.

"Seems like it wouldn't be another cake," Mom says.

"Or a pie." Scott hands me a twenty. "Lunch is on me, champ."

I tuck the bill in my pocket. "Thanks. Yeah. I'm thinking something French."

"Croissants?" Elly guesses.

I shudder. "Oh my frog. I sure hope not." Then I think. "It won't be that. Not enough time."

"Speaking of which, it's past time for lunch. I'm famished." Elly grabs my arm.

"You are always famished." Rajit zips his hoodie.

"Growing girl and all that." Elly tugs us both toward the door.

"Rexi and I are ready to go," adds Wayne.

"Be back at one!" Scott calls.

Elly holds up her phone. "I've set a timer! No way we're missing the grand finale."

A gust of wind blasts us as we step outside. I shrivel up in my jacket. "It's freezing!"

"We'll walk fast." Elly picks up the pace.

"You're probably extra cold because you've been doing all that baking." Rajit steps closer to share some body heat.

"I hope there's Korean." Wayne pauses to let Rexi sniff a scraggly daffodil.

"There's anything you want. See, we're already here!" Elly leads us around a square dotted with food trucks. We check them all out and then order.

"All these amazing foods and you pick plain old fried rice?" Elly shakes her head at me as she dives into her gyro.

"Don't judge. Besides, hardly plain old. This has cilantro! And chicken! And at least two veggies." Each bite is a pajama party in my mouth. We top off our lunches with a quick walk over to the Pearl District, which warms us up enough to enjoy ice cream from Cool Moon.

"Okay, I thought cardamom would be strange but . . ." Elly takes another lick of her cone. "Where has it been all my life?"

"Nothing beats this pumpkin." Rajit practically purrs.

"Rocky Road is the best." Wayne licks chocolate from his fingers. "Poor Rexi can't have any. Chocolate is bad for dogs."

"Sorbet all the way." I wave my cone. "And marionberry is the unofficial fruit of Oregon."

Elly's phone pings with a reminder. "We better book. Twenty minutes till showtime."

Our stroll turns into a fast walk; I hit an uneven spot on the sidewalk. "Ouch!"

Wayne catches me.

"You okay?" Rajit asks.

"Missed my step. Kind of jarring." I rub my side.

Elly whips out her phone. "Should I call an Uber?"

"Don't freak. It was just, surprising." I inhale, visualizing breath traveling to and through my gut. "I'm fine. Really." I say this as much for myself as for them. Maybe all that rice was a dumb idea. And sometimes there's dairy in sorbet, too. I should've asked.

At the hotel, I pause at the main doors. Can I finish another round?

"Ready to do this?" Elly punches me in the arm.

"Oyster sauce breath. Gotta brush. See you in there." The elevator feels stuffy after the crisp outside air. I peel off my jacket and wipe sweat beads from my lip. As soon as the car door opens, I dash to my room. I fish the Imodium out of my toiletries bag and swallow down two caplets before brushing my teeth. My stomach is still not happy, so I pop a couple Tums, too. I should've skipped lunch! Stuck with a protein shake.

I reapply deodorant, brush my hair, and roll on some lip gloss. I stick a cold washcloth on the back of my neck and leave it there until it's time to go.

This time I share the elevator with an older couple. The lady reminds me of Mrs. Medcalf.

"Aren't you one of the bakers?" she asks.

She takes my nod as an invitation to keep talking. "It's astonishing what you kids are doing. Why, I didn't even know what ganache was at your age."

I should say something to be polite. "Do you have someone in the bake-off?"

"Our grandson, Simon." The man clucks his tongue. "That imposter challenge did him in. But you should try his Creamsicle macarons."

"Sounds really good." An ember flares in my gut. "Oh!" The much-too-familiar flick startles me. No. Please no. I press on my ring.

"Yes?" The lady smiles expectantly.

Wing it. "Um. Could you ask Simon to hang around after? So I can get his recipe?" The first flick is followed by another and another. I rock to dodge the pain. But there is no dodging. The Knife's relentless.

"You go ahead, dear." The man holds the door for me. "You've got baking to do!"

I dash for the green room toilet, turning on the fan so no one can hear. But nothing happens, aside from the stabbing pain. I wash my hands and join Flora and Finn.

"You two are doing great. Enjoy this last challenge," Finn advises.

Flora pulls on her apron. "Do you feel all right?" She stops in mid-tie, worry on her face.

I roll a chilled water bottle along my forehead. "Overheated. That's all."

Finn mumbles something into their headpiece then looks at us. "Ready."

"Good luck, Tess."

"You too." My arms feel like ice sculptures as I tie my apron. You'd think the heat in my gut would melt them, but they are frozen, useless lumps hooked to my shoulders. I wobble to my workstation, resting my hip against the counter to keep upright. The people in the audience bob around like rubber duckies in Gracie's bath.

There are three people at the judges' station. Do I have double vision? I blink. No, definitely three people. Then I remember that Mr. Kenton from Jubilee Flour is helping with this final round.

Chef Marie's instructions get stuck in the mush that's

my brain; my head grows heavier and heavier as she speaks. Not sure I can hold it up.

Somehow the word *éclair* lands on the one small dot of my brain that's still functioning.

"Woot! Éclairs!" Elly hollers loud enough to be heard over the crowd noise. "You've got this!"

I blink hard. Tune in. Do I have this?

Chef Marie turns toward Deke. "And in addition to a dozen éclairs," he says, "we want you to bake one dozen cream puffs, half stuffed with sweet filling and half with savory. Here's your chance to really show your chops." He rubs his hands together.

"On behalf of Jubilee Flour, I wish you both the best of luck." Mr. Kenton's smile is encouraging and kind.

"Ready, set," starts Chef Marie.

"Bake!" hollers Deke.

The Knife pounces when I bend down to grab the flour. I try to deal, but it overpowers me and I crumple to the floor. Even curled in the fetal position, I can't protect myself from the stabbing pain.

"Tess?" Chef Marie crouches down.

"Medic!" Deke hollers. In a flash, the EMT's kneeling, fishing a stethoscope from her kit. "Can you tell me what's going on?"

Another stab. I gasp. "I have Crohn's. Having a flare."

Mom's stroking my head. "You're going to be okay."

I tell the EMT about the Tums and the Imodium. "Can I have some water?"

Chef Marie hands me a bottle. "Mr. Kenton, please call for a ten-minute break."

On the floor, behind the workstation, I hear the ups and downs of Mr. Kenton's voice, not his words. But the audience responds with a sympathetic groan. A head pops over the counter.

"Now you're a drama queen, huh?" Elly reaches out her hand. I grab it.

"Yeah. Not enough attention, I guess." I gasp again.

"What can we do to help you finish?" Chef Marie asks.

"We could turn off the lights. Get you a runner. Whatever it takes, we'll make it happen." Deke drums his fingers on the countertop.

I lean my head on Mom's. What would it take to make this happen? More than a ten-minute break. My body's drenched in sweat. I shift to ease the pain in my left side.

"You've got a real shot here," Deke says.

I know he's right. I do. I could win this for Dad.

Flora hugs herself. "Can I help?"

Chef Marie hands over a cold cloth, which Mom places on the back of my neck.

"I'm sorry to put pressure on," Mr. Kenton says. "But

we need to start up again soon or we won't have time to complete this round."

Now Elly's on the floor next to me. "Jimi Hendrix. Remember?"

I remember. Something about an unfinished album. Like this competition is unfinished work for me. A chance to make it right for Dad. No, for me. I struggle to sit up. "Can I get a sports drink? And maybe some saltines?"

In seconds, I'm crunching crackers and washing them down with fluorescent yellow liquid. The three judges confer and suggest Elly stay up here, to help me. Flora's on board with it. Which is classy of her. I finish the crackers and stand up. Brace myself against the workstation.

"You can do this," Elly says.

"You can," Flora adds. Flora! Rooting for me.

I smooth out my apron and reach for a canister. The crowd bursts into applause. Wayne's cheering and Rexi's barking. So many people on my side. I can do this. Panting, I scoop out flour for Elly to weigh. "150 grams," I tell her. We weigh the water, butter, salt. And Dad's secret ingredient: 8 grams of sugar.

"Want me to stir?" Elly reaches for the spoon. But this isn't something for a beginner.

"You could put *that* on the burner." I point, hoping it sounds like I'm trying to give her something to do and not like I can't lift the saucepan myself. I don't have to do much stirring while everything melts together so I rest against the counter. When everything simmers, I dump in the measured flour.

I sweep the wooden spoon around the saucepan, sweating after each rotation. It's never going to form a ball at this rate. Every stroke rips something more out of me. I've still got to beat in the eggs. Pipe the éclairs. There's no way—

Stop it, Tess. How many times have you made éclairs? You can do this.

I take a shaky swig of water while gathering my strength to dump the dough into the mixer.

I *have* to do this. I've worked so hard to be here. I have to do it for myself. For Dad.

"Tess," Elly whispers. She nods at the clock, which is ticking as fast as my heart. "What's next?"

I swallow hard. "Can you break four eggs into that?" She does and hands me the plastic deli container holding about 260 grams of slick whites and orangey yolks. 260 grams. About what a kitten weighs. Eighty pennies. Or a cup of sugar. I should be able to lift that.

Should be able to. The container wobbles as I grip it. Flora's already piping her éclairs. I need to get a move on.

The container clunks on the countertop. I close my eyes. Feel Elly's hand on my shoulder. She gets it.

I'm out of juice. An expired battery.

Even with Elly, I can't do this.

From somewhere I hear Dad's voice: *Good baking is the chemistry between ingredients and the cook.*

I press my dandelion ring. *Oh, Dad, I'm so sorry.* I don't have it right now. That chemistry. The Knife's in the way. Messing things up.

I glance around. My family. Chef Marie. Even Flora. All sending me good vibes to see this through. But it's not enough.

I rub my wet face with my apron. All I want to do is sit down. Lie down.

Then I catch a whiff of Doublemint. It's like an arm around me. Not nudging me forward but holding me in place. Supporting me.

No matter what.

I grab Elly's hand again. "I need to go home," I say.

She squeezes. One-two-three. Quick learner.

Chef Marie accepts my decision graciously. She, Deke, and Mr. Kenton put their heads together and decide to continue with the final round, inviting both Maren and Alpana to compete with Flora.

We are somewhere north of Centralia and I'm drifting off to sleep in the back of Mom's SUV when my phone pings.

> Maren killed it with her bake: éclairs with peanut butter mousse, cream puffs with lemon curd, and the savory ones with rosemary chicken paté. I got to try one and it was scrummy!

Elly types in about a dozen exclamation points.

> She deserves the win. 🖤

> Guess what? Her dad drives to Seattle once a month. I told her she needs to come with. Sleepover!

I text a smiley face back, and, after a sip of the ginger ale Scott bought me, plug in my headphones. Dial a number I've been texting all this year and listen to a voice I love: "Tony here. Leave me a message to make my dreams crumb true." Dad and his dorky puns. He never could've guessed how true this message is. He *is* here. No matter how many cracks there are in my heart, he'll never slip through.

I squeeze my eyes shut, hit redial, and listen a couple more times. I remember asking him once why he became a baker. He said it wasn't any one thing, that there were lots of reasons. I wished I'd asked him what all those reasons were.

Weirdly, Mrs. Chatterjee's essay pops into my mind, and I finally get why I've had such a hard time with it. She's looking for one thing that makes you who you are. But there is no one thing, like Dad said. He and I come from the world of recipes, where a bunch of ingredients get stirred together to make something wonderful, like a life. Even a wonky one like mine. I smile in the dark. I might be condemned to another purple C minus, but I finally know what I'm going to write about.

A sticky hand pats my arm. "Are you asleep, Tessie?"

"Yes."

Gracie giggles. "Then how come you're talking?"

Mom leans around the seat. "Let your sister rest."

"It's okay." I take Gracie's hand. Pump it three times. She squeezes back. "Dad taught us that, right?"

I turn to watch the full moon following us home. "Yes. Yes, he did."

Chapter 26

On the last day of school, Rajit and I linger outside the gym doors with a bunch of other kids looking like they might bolt, too.

"Ready?" Rajit tugs at his shirt collar.

The pulsing bass batters on the gym doors, threatening to shove them open. Is that butterflies in my stomach? Or something else? Something sharp? "Elly probably won't even notice if we no-show," I say.

"Right. She's so busy running everything and stuff." He messes with his hair. "Who are we kidding? She'd kill us."

Deep breath. Check in like Dr. Lee taught me. Quick mental scan of the innards. Butterflies. Definitely butter-flies. I recite the message Elly wrote on that napkin: *"You must do the thing you think you cannot do."* I hold up my hand for a high five. "I mean, if Eleanor Roosevelt said it, it must be true."

"Abso-freakin-lootely." He yanks open the door and the undertow of energy from a couple hundred pumped-up eighth graders sucks us inside. Rajit lets out a whoop and grabs my hand. "Let's do this!"

I whoop, too. Across the floor, I spot Elly and Wayne laughing and springing, up-down, up-down, up-down, to the beat. Rajit pushes me in their direction, and we somehow slide through the crowd.

"Tessie!" Elly and I do our brand-new signature move, the one we invented special for today. Rajit rolls his eyes, but Wayne tries to copy us. We hop around, making absolute fools of ourselves. When the song stops, we all stand, arm in arm, panting to catch our breath before the next song starts.

The DJ spins the next track and Elly screams. Even the kids who've been standing on the edges pour out onto the floor. I'm bouncing with Elly and Rajit and Wayne. Warm and light. Like a balloon. Or a feather. Or like a normal kid. Emmett waves at me from across the room, behind Tenley's back. I wave, too. We're taking Ruffles to visit Mabel again tomorrow. I'm bringing killer Morning Glory muffins; gotta be true to my Ms. Bread Science persona. And maybe this time, I'll tell him some things about Dad. Emmett may have questionable taste in girlfriends, but he's a good listener.

"Hey, you!" Elly grabs my hand and we fake some fifties dance moves. I laugh. Make up another new goofy turn.

"Are you having fun?" she hollers.

"Yes!!" And it's true. I'm having a blast. Okay, so I may need to find the bathroom after this dance. But it's okay.

Rajit can't eat popcorn because of his braces. Brooklyn goes to the nurse every day for her insulin. Wayne needs Rexi. Even Elly the indestructible hyperventilates over spiders.

The music stops and I let go of Elly's hand. "Back in a sec," I tell her.

"You okay?"

Thumbs-up. More than okay. "Sometimes a girl's just gotta go."

"Get some water while you're out there."

"Yes, Mom."

She pokes her tongue out and then shrieks, "Oh, my favorite song!" Now Dylan's in front of her and they are jumping together, grinning like models in toothpaste ads.

On my way back from the bathroom, I pass Mrs. Chatterjee's class. She waves me in, her bracelets jingling. "Tess! Your essay is wonderful. Very fresh. And courageous of you to be so honest."

"Thank you."

"Did you know I'm also the advisor for the high school student newspaper? Always looking for reporters. Would you consider taking journalism in the fall?"

"You must be desperate."

"I won't say we're overrun with writers. But not desperate." Her bracelets tinkle cheerily. "Given your interests, perhaps a column on baking?"

"Like recipes?"

Her hands move back and forth, a small symphony of bracelet music. "If that's what interests you."

I can't help myself. "Maybe a baking challenge?"

"Oh, I love *Iron Chef*." She smiles. "Could be fun."

My mind's already whirring. Best cupcake made with a vegetable. Cookies with five ingredients. A dessert with no sugar. "I'll think about it."

Brooklyn's waiting outside the classroom; she nods as I pass by. "I took your advice."

"Advice?"

"Honey." She holds out an armful of books. "I'm planning to catch some flies."

"I loved that one." *You Bring the Distant Near* by Mitali Perkins is right on top.

She pats the stack. "This is my version of the old-fashioned apple for the teacher."

I grin. "Evil kid genius takes over the world."

"I'll settle for Language Arts class." Brooklyn tucks the books under her arm. "Once she reads these, she's gotta see there's more than Jane Austen. Even if it's too late for us."

"Lifting up the younger generation?" I ask.

"Something like that." She shifts the books in her arms. "Just doing my part."

"You should come down. To the dance," I say.

"First things first. Wish me luck. I'm going in." She straightens her shoulders then strides into the classroom.

I peek around the doorframe. Mrs. Chatterjee takes the books. Invites Brooklyn to sit. And she's smiling. They both are.

On the way back to the gym, I spot a new poster: IT ALWAYS SEEMS IMPOSSIBLE UNTIL IT IS DONE. —NELSON MANDELA.

The man was in jail for twenty-seven years. In a cell that was three paces, wall to wall. With a lightbulb blaring day and night. He's got the cred. And I agree: Prison. The Knife. Giving up is not an option.

So maybe I will always need to keep tabs on the nearest bathroom. Deal with flare-ups. Leave sleepovers early. I might even have to ask for some accommodations at school. I have a disease; I'm not a disease.

I'm a girl. With dreams. With friends waiting downstairs at a dance.

And a powerful craving to bake a huge batch of Joyful Cookies.

Finally! I get to hear what Tess thinks!

Tess Medina
LA 4th Period, Chatterjee
Final Essay

My Most Defining Moment

I am writing this essay based on the assigned prompt, but, no offense, it's impossible to pick only one defining moment and describe what I learned from it, even for someone who's only fourteen. I sure can't, so I will write about four.

Defining moment number one: chocolate cake. On my fifth birthday, when I stood on the stool at the kitchen counter with my dad, I felt more powerful than Harry Potter. I could perform magic with eggs, milk, flour, sugar!

But baking isn't about magic. It's about rules. That's one reason I love baking: The rules pay off. Here are the basics:

1) Bakers use scales, not measuring cups.
2) There are three main principles: Sugar equals flour, eggs plus liquid equal sugar, eggs also equal butter. I could explain in detail, but I'm going to ask you to trust me on this.
3) Share what you bake.

Defining moment number two: my dad's death. Remember when you asked for an example of "resolute" in class that one time? If you'd called on me, I would've said my dad. I see his face every time I unwrap a stick of gum, the vice he subbed out for cigarettes. He exercised and ate kale even though he hated it. (Kale, not exercise.)

It turns out following rules doesn't always pay off. One day, Dad and I are at my first-ever baking competition, and the next, I'm wearing a black dress and shaking hands with strangers who promised that time would heal all. Trust me: Broken hearts stay broken.

Defining moment number three: the Knife, aka Crohn's disease. Did you know there are twenty-five feet of intestines squished inside each of us? And Crohn's can mess with each and every inch. Bonus: no cure.

I'm sure when you made your rules about bathroom passes, you weren't thinking about Crohn's. I wouldn't have, either. Until recently, I'd never heard the word before. Never gave a thought to my colon. Who does?

Crohn's is a piece of (four-letter word) and it's not c-a-k-e. I know certain things are not discussed in proper society (do I get credit for this reference to Jane Austen?), but "Any blood or mucus in your stools?" is a question I've had to answer more times than you've sent Loki Marshall to the VP's office.

Most girls would rather die than use school bathrooms. Not an option for me. I pray every time that no one can hear me. Or smell me. Imagine you've always been able to handle pizza but, one day, it goes off like a time bomb in your gut. And you have no idea where the nearest bathroom is. This is something I don't have to imagine.

Defining moment number four: the Jubilee Flour 10th Anniversary Bake-Off. Not to brag, but how many kids have made it to the Jubilee Flour Bake-Off finals twice?

The first competition with Dad was a grade-A defining moment. The second competition was also grade-A. Not because I won, but because I withdrew. After making it to the final round. The Knife didn't win, though. That was all me. Carpe diem. I seized the day and did what needed to be done. Crohn's may make a lot of noise, but Tess is leading this parade.

Northlake prides itself on its motivational posters. What we need is one with a quote from the movie *Super 8*, where Joe tells the alien: "I know bad things happen. Bad things happen. But you can still live. You can still live."

Because no one moment defines you.

That's the only message a middle schooler needs to hear.

The End

A LETTER FROM KIRBY AND QUINN

Quinn, age 14,
courtesy of the authors

Kirby and Quinn; Mother's Day
2019, courtesy of the authors

WHY WOULD WE WANT TO WRITE A STORY
ABOUT A YOUNG GIRL WITH CROHN'S DISEASE?

Quinn: My earliest memories include stomachaches. Even as a really small child, I remember pain in my abdomen and urgently needing the bathroom. For many years it was chalked up to my being nervous or to something I'd eaten. At least, those were the explanations the doctors gave us. It wasn't until my early teens, when my symptoms began to take full form, that we grew determined to discover the true answer behind what was going on. We made desperate trips to one specialist and then to another and another and another. With each specialist the diagnosis shifted. It was exhausting and discouraging. After years of searching, failed medications and treatments, and fighting to make my voice heard, I finally found a physician who actually listened to me and understood that, though my lab work might appear "normal," I was indeed sick. He gave a diagnosis of Crohn's disease, prescribing proper treatments that finally began to work. We are so grateful to that doctor, Dr. Scott D. Lee of UW Medicine, that we named Tess's doctor in his honor.

What I have come to learn about living with this disease is that it's a journey, a long road with no end (no cure as of yet) and lots of twists and turns. You can be in remission for months, almost forgetting you have Crohn's, and then everything suddenly comes crashing down. Perhaps a previously reliable treatment stops working and so the search for another begins. I have also learned that while having Crohn's disease sometimes impacts the things I do, it does not define who I am: a proud woman, wife, mother, daughter, friend, and chocolate lover, who also happens to have Crohn's.

If you are just learning of your diagnosis, do find a support system and know that there is always, always hope that better is around the corner.

Kirby: It was incredibly difficult watching my beloved teenaged daughter struggle as we tried to find out what was "wrong" with her. And frustrating because she experienced what many girls and women do: dismissive attitudes from health professionals. Like Tess, Quinn's undiagnosed illness kept her from enjoying many fun activities—hanging out with friends, going to dances, eating the occasional junk food. Like Tess, Quinn's illness made her different, and sometimes even her closest friends lacked empathy and understanding for her situation. Like Tess, Quinn has always been a trouper.

As Quinn mentions above, it took a very long time to find help (thankfully, there is more awareness about the IBD family of diseases today). Dr. Scott D. Lee was the first physician to look beyond the lab reports and provide Quinn with an accurate diagnosis. I clearly remember the day we first met with him, sobbing out of sheer gratitude that, finally, someone listened.

While I've had the honor of coauthoring other books, writing with my daughter is better than an unlimited supply of sea salt caramels. Quinn is patient where I am not and wise beyond her years. I am in awe of her bravery in recalling painful times and committing those memories to the page. And without Quinn, Tess would never have texted her dad—a brilliant suggestion inspired by my mom, who still keeps my dad's cell phone active so the family can hear his voice mail message whenever we need to.

Quinn and Kirby: We applaud the burgeoning efforts of literature to normalize conversations about physical and mental health realities and issues. By writing a hopeful, honest, and sometimes humorous story of living with Crohn's disease, it is our hope to add to that conversation. We also want to support the Quinns and Tesses of the world dealing with various hard-to-talk-about conditions—from alopecia to vitiligo—by saying it's okay to talk, even about the embarrassing stuff. And for those blessedly unaffected by physical or mental health challenges, we hope this story offers insights that may foster greater understanding, empathy, and kindness.

GENERAL INFORMATION ABOUT CROHN'S DISEASE

This story focuses on Crohn's, one disease of a larger group called IBD. IBD—which stands for inflammatory bowel disease—is an umbrella term used to describe disorders that cause chronic inflammation of the gastrointestinal tract. The two most common forms of IBD are Crohn's disease (more common in females) and ulcerative colitis, or UC (more common in males).

Research has shown a rise in the number of young people dealing with IBD. According to the American College of Gastroenterology, about 75,000 teenagers develop inflammatory bowel disease (IBD) each year, including UC and Crohn's disease.

While the cause is not really understood, scientists know that it involves an interaction between genes, the immune system, and environmental factors. Normally, the immune system attacks foreign invaders to keep the body healthy. In people with IBD, the immune system attacks healthy cells, causing inflammation and illness.

Individual symptoms vary, but common ones include diarrhea, abdominal pain, rectal bleeding, urgent need to move bowels, fever, loss of appetite, nausea, weight loss, fatigue, night sweats, and loss of normal menstrual cycle.

While there is not a cure for Crohn's, there are many treatment options that can be used to bring the disease into remission. If you have any of the symptoms listed, talk to your doctor. An early diagnosis is key to getting this disease under control.

To learn more, visit the Crohn's & Colitis Foundation, crohnscolitisfoundation.org.

ACKNOWLEDGMENTS

Kirby & Quinn: As always with a novel, the list of thank-yous is long: much gratitude to Ainsley Olesen for insights about middle school, to Mary Nethery for character development suggestions, and to first readers Sunshine Bacon, Dori Hillestad Butler, and Linda Johns. Special shout out to Linda for the spot-on title.

We are incredibly grateful to agent extraordinaire Jill Grinberg and her head of operations, Denise Page for patiently nudging us to find the true essence of this story and for championing our work with enormous passion.

Our Scholastic family has whole-heartedly embraced this book; we are moved by their acceptance and commitment. Lisa Sandell, as ever, is a dream editor. Thank you to Ellie Berger, David Levithan, Janell Harris, book designer Cassy Price, Aleah Gornbein, Rachel Feld, Katie Dutton, Seale Ballenger, Erin Berger, Lizette Serrano, Emily Heddleson, the fabulous Scholastic sales team, Maisha Johnson, Sabrina Montenigro, Michael Strouse, Meredith Wardell, Chris Stengel, Elizabeth Parisi, Lori Benton, John Pels, and to Book Fairs and Book Clubs.

Kirby: My biggest thanks go to Quinn, who has long wanted to write this book. She endured my reluctance to revisit that tough time in our lives with her typical grace; but she persisted and prevailed. She is brave every single day and especially in sharing her story here. Love you, Bug.

Quinn: My first gratitude goes to my mom, Kirby Larson. From day one she has believed there was a better way and supported me on my journey. Without her talent, this novel would never have happened.

I am very thankful for my husband, Matthew Wyatt, who has supported me unconditionally in this process and in both sickness and in health.

I want to also thank Lisa Sandell and the Scholastic family for seeing the heart of this story and being brave enough to share about topics that may not always be the easiest to discuss.

ABOUT THE AUTHORS

Quinn Wyatt lives in Kenmore, Washington, with her two wonderful daughters, fabulous husband, and so-so dog. She loves to grow things in her garden, learn new crafting techniques, volunteer at her kids' school, and bake yummy things (especially with chocolate). Quinn has lived with Crohn's for most of her life and is encouraged by all of the progress that has been made over the years in the treatment of Inflammatory Bowel Diseases.

Kirby Larson is the acclaimed author of the Newbery Honor book *Hattie Big Sky*; its sequel, *Hattie Ever After*; the history-mysteries *Audacity Jones to the Rescue* and *Audacity Jones Steals the Show*; *The Friendship Doll*; The Dogs of WWII series, including *Dash* (winner of the Scott O'Dell Award for Historical Fiction), *Duke*, *Liberty*, and *Code Word Courage*; and the Shermy and Shake series. She's also co-written two award-winning picture books: *Two Bobbies: A True Story of Hurricane Katrina, Friendship, and Survival* and *Nubs: The True Story of a Mutt, a Marine & a Miracle*. Kirby lives in Washington state with her husband, Neil, and their very naughty dog, Raleigh.